MW00358810

Flotsam

Praise for Flotsam

"With compassion and urgency, Patricia Boomsma's *Flotsam* depicts the deep and raw grief of a community damaged by the disappearance of some of its most vulnerable members. Told through a variety of perspectives and with a solid foundation of understanding and knowledge, this novel does not shy away from scathing commentary on losses dangerously ignored. At its heart, though, *Flotsam* is a story of mothers and daughters and the yearning toward a better system of care and concern for those most in need." — Patricia Ann McNair, *Responsible Adults*

Bink Books
Bedazzled Ink Publishing Company • Fairfield, California

© 2023 Patricia Boomsma

All rights reserved. No part of this publication may be reproduced or transmitted in any means, electronic or mechanical, without permission in writing from the publisher.

This is a work of fiction. Names, characters, businesses, places, events, locales, and incidents are either the products of the author's imagination or used in a fictitious manner. Any resemblance to actual persons, living or dead, or to actual events is purely coincidental.

Content Guidance: This is a crime fiction novel that includes subject matter which some people may find distressing, including violence, post-traumatic stress, opioid addiction, suicide, and many missing and murdered indigenous people. Please read with care.

978-1-960373-12-0 paperback

Cover Design
by
Sapling Studio

Bink Books
a division of
Bedazzled Ink Publishing, LLC
Fairfield, California
http://www.bedazzledink.com

*For the many missing and murdered Indigenous people
and all those who love and miss them.*

A WHIFF OF sulfur burned Traveler's muzzle. The whistle and crack of explosions pained his tall ears as bursts of color lit the night sky. He ran along the river until he heard only night noises—water falling, dried grass rattling, an owl hooting, a flurry of bats. Then he sat howling for his brothers. He'd wandered many rivers since they'd last answered.

The smell of smoke and meat lured Traveler toward a jumble of human noise. He crept along the edges of the trees to where the scent was strongest and people moved in and out of the unnatural light. A blot of darkness moved from the light inside a shelter and tossed a large black bag toward a row of cans overflowing with the stench of food. Traveler inched closer, then crouched in the shadows when the hulk turned.

Traveler's ears twitched at the sound of a car door opening and closing.

A man walked toward the light, his arms around a woman whose long, straight hair fell forward, hiding her darkened face.

"What happened? She's not much use to us like this," the hulk said in a tone that would have made Traveler run if he weren't so hungry. "Just enough to relax them, make them happy, is what I said."

"She was going to leave," the other man said. "She'd already seen us."

Traveler tensed his body, ready to bolt.

"OK, bring her in, put her in the downstairs bedroom. I know a couple of guys who ain't too picky about their girls."

The ground darkened, and Traveler calmed when the door closed. He braced his paws on the lip of a can and tore at the plastic inside until it ripped open. The sudden intensity and wealth of smells excited Traveler to push his nose deep, and the can clattered to the ground. He stopped and looked toward the building, but no one came. He devoured scorched meat and bread soggy with fat and tomato, then returned to the forest.

ONE

MONDAY, JUNE 16, 2014

KELLY FLYNN TRIPPED on a frayed section of the hallway's worn beige carpeting, distracted as she rehearsed her argument for this afternoon's hearing. *Pay attention.* She remembered now why she seldom wore spike heels. She hurried past the scuffed office doors of other attorneys huddled over their cluttered desks. Clara looked up and smiled, gave Kelly a small wave, and returned to staring at her computer screen. The red rug and bright paintings of sunflowers made Clara's office a welcome bit of color from the hallway's blank white walls and the beige functionality of most of the offices.

I should do more to brighten my office. Kelly hung her black raincoat on the hook behind her office door. Diplomas and awards and a picture of herself with Justice Ginsburg taken at a charitable dinner at a conference in DC filled Kelly's walls. Books and overflowing accordion files filled the bookshelves that lined two sides of the room, and stacks of loose papers, pens, and pencils surrounded a picture of Ruth and a computer on her desk. She grimaced at the thought of decorating. She never even took the time to clear off her desk, preferring to have whatever she was working on near at hand. Carmen, the office manager, often complained that if anything happened to Kelly, no one would be able to find anything. Probably true, but who had time to organize?

She dropped into her chair, trying to decide which of the many scattered files she should pick up first, dreading another morning of the sad cases that made their way through her office. So many in pain, forgotten by those who preferred tax cuts to social services and ravaged by a judicial system that favored the wealthy and took too long to help anyone in crisis. She often felt like that little Dutch boy trying to hold back the sea wall with his thumb.

She knew which finger she'd use.

Carmen leaned on the doorjamb, a set of keys dangling from her freckled hand. "Good morning. Somebody found a floating foot along Galmenberg Bay. Boss wants you to head out there."

"A what?" Kelly asked.

"You know, a shoe with a foot in it, like the ones they keep finding in Canada."

"OK. But why do I need to drive out to the sticks to see it?"

"There's an issue of jurisdiction."

Kelly grumbled to herself about needing to get ready for her hearing, but took off her heels, put on the gym shoes she kept in a drawer, and gave Carmen a sideways smile as she slipped the key ring past the Carmen's long red fingernail. Carmen towered over Kelly's smaller, softer body, but Carmen's self-confidence, not her size, subdued Kelly and almost everyone in the office, even the new prosecuting attorneys that changed every four to eight years. Kelly shrugged her coat back on and trudged down the stairs to the underground garage where the office parked its Caprice, an old police cruiser repainted and repurposed for a government pool car.

The morning fog was a bolster of gray along the horizon as Kelly drove toward the coast. She tried to recall what she knew about the spate of floating feet discovered along the Pacific shoreline the past few years. Not much. For years, the bones beach walkers found inside a hiking boot or running shoe had been British Columbia's problem. Then the feet started showing up in Washington. The media loved them, asked whether a serial killer was at work. Copycats soon followed: pig bones, even a bear claw, stuffed into a shoe. Most couldn't be identified, and those that were turned out not to be murder victims.

Kelly rolled down her window as she neared the bay to feel the cool June breeze. She loved the constant rush of the waves, the briny sea air that reminded her to be glad she'd left the diesel and factory smells of the South Chicago neighborhood where she'd grown up. She parked between the medical examiner's gray van and a black and white SUV with *Sheriff* emblazoned in gold. A strong ocean wind lifted her hair from behind her ears and into her eyes as she passed an old blue van marked *Nininpak Nation* and followed the increasing roar of waves down a steep path toward the yellow tape.

Twigs, pine needles, and bright red leaves littered the rocks, sand, and tide pools along the shore. She licked the salt on her lips and wiped the sea spray from her glasses. She nodded to a kneeling man in a khaki green uniform with the name *Springer* embroidered on his shirt. He stopped taking pictures and stood. Young, clean shaven, and sunburnt, his tall, fit body dominated her view. His eyes hid behind reflective sunglasses, but the line of his narrow mouth told Kelly something irritated him.

"Hi, I'm Kelly Flynn from the prosecuting attorney's office. You asked for us?"

Deputy Springer lifted his camera as a greeting and pointed it toward a group of women talking with a man in the dark blue uniform Kelly recognized as the Nininpak Tribal Police. "Sheriff thought we needed somebody." He shrugged as if he didn't. "Those women were crabbing and called tribal police when they found the shoe. He called us because he thinks the Reservation ends around sixty yards north of here. Talk to him."

Kelly looked north, wondering if they thought she knew where the boundary line lay. If it became important, they'd get the surveyors out. Springer crouched back into the shallow water next to a log sheltering rotting leaves, a dead fish, and a black trainer covered with strings of seaweed. Dr. Green, the county medical examiner, bent over the shoe, her gray coveralls wet above her black waders and along her arms. She used a long-handled screwdriver to prod open a dirty white sock stuffed in the shoe.

"I suppose it was inevitable we'd get one," Dr. Green said, then looked up at Kelly. "Good to see you, Ms. Flynn. It's been a while."

"Can't assume much from a gym shoe and a sock," Kelly said.

"Nope." Dr. Green folded open the sock with her gloved hands to peer at the bone. "Human," she said as she put the shoe into an evidence bag.

"Time of death?" Kelly asked, putting on a somber face.

Dr. Green looked at Kelly, smiled, and shook her head. It was their shtick ever since they met at an employee picnic years ago and bonded over the brilliance of television coroners who could glance at a body and know. *Wish I'd gone to their medical school,* Dr. Green had said.

"I'll try to figure out when this shoe was made and sold," Springer said, stuffing his camera into its case.

Kelly turned toward the silent women staring at the waves.

Springer raised his arm and shouted, "Officer Sweka," over the waves crashing ever closer. The Nininpak officer waved them over. He had an intensity his angular features and crisp blue uniform only emphasized. Kelly and Springer stepped over the rocks along the shoreline toward the sandy part of the beach.

"Thanks for calling us," Springer said, thrusting his hand toward Sweka when they reached the silent group. "My name is Springer, and this here is Ms. Flynn. Is there a boundary marker?"

Sweka grasped, then dropped Springer's hand. "Daniel Sweka," he said, nodding to Kelly. "The Nation includes the banks of the Hotsaem River where it meets Galmenberg Bay, including that part that juts out over there."

He pointed to a thin peninsula of land between the River and the Bay. "We're well past that."

"We didn't know we'd gone too far," the oldest of the three women said.

"It's fine," Kelly said to her. "It's all public land along this part of the Bay. The boundary just helps us decide who investigates."

"I assume you got statements?" Springer asked.

"Yes. I'll send you copies when they're typed, but I'm sure you want to talk to them, too." Sweka smiled encouragingly at a young woman whose long black hair spilled in a thick strand from the elasticized opening in the back of a ball cap embroidered with a stylized swooping bird. "Margarete saw the shoe first."

Margarete glanced at Springer, looked down, nodded, and clenched her hands.

"Hi, Margarete. I'm Deputy Springer of the Cascadia County Sheriff's Office. May I ask you a few questions?"

Margarete nodded.

"How did you come across the shoe?" he asked.

"We were fishing for crabs." Margarete waved her hand toward a large bucket filled with melting ice and three large crabs. "When I saw the shoe with a sock, I poked at it with my stick. Something was in it, so I lifted it up and saw the bone inside. We called the tribal police and Daniel came."

"Did you meet any runners or other walkers this morning?"

Margarete pointed to the bluff a few hundred feet from the shore. "I saw a guy on the ridge this morning while we were waiting, but not here on the beach."

"Did you come past the same place yesterday?"

"No."

As Springer talked with Margarete, Kelly looked at the other women. All wore clear ponchos over their clothes and heavy black plastic boots that reached mid-calf. One woman wore jeans and a puffy vest, her hair tied back with a pink scrunchie, and the other, older woman, wore a loose dress cinched at the waist with a woven belt and a wide-brimmed straw hat atop her long, graying hair. The older woman scanned the beach and the sea as she twisted the ends of her belt in her hands. Together they watched the white caps grow as the tide rolled in.

When Springer finished talking with Margarete, Sweka introduced the young woman as Liz and the older as Therese.

"Did either of you see anything?" Springer asked.

They shook their heads.

"I walked here last week and didn't see anything then," Therese said. "I was with my dog and he would have found it."

Springer nodded. "Thank you. If I need to talk with you again, how can I reach you?"

"My daughter's missing," Therese blurted, her eyes and forehead tight with worry. "Could it be her?"

A zing of fear shot through Kelly. She'd attended a continuing legal education seminar on missing women six months ago, and the stark and frightening statistics chilled her. To meet a mother of a missing girl made these statistics all too real, too close. She shivered, thinking about her daughter Ruth's late nights out who-knows-where.

"Do you recognize the shoe?" Springer asked.

"No, but she's been living in Galmenberg a couple of years now, so I don't know for sure."

"How long has she been missing?" Kelly asked.

"I'm not sure. Daniel says he saw her at a party at the Casino on Memorial Day." Therese pointed to Sweka, and he nodded.

"Then I don't think so," Springer said. "The bone looks pretty clean. That takes more than a couple of weeks."

"Will you help me find her?" Therese had a pleading sadness in her eyes as she looked first at Springer and then at Kelly.

"Have you filed a missing person's report?" Springer asked.

Therese stiffened. "Of course I did. And posted flyers. Tribal police are helping me but say because she lived off the Reservation, there's not much they can do."

Sweka grimaced.

"Galmenberg police don't do nothing," Therese said. "Say she's an adult so her being missing isn't a crime. But something's happened to her. I know it."

"I posted her picture on Facebook," Margarete said, flashing her phone in Kelly's face. "Lots of people hope we find her, but nobody's posted anything about seeing her lately."

Kelly looked at Sweka. *Ah, this is the real issue.* Adult missing person cases could be hard. People ran away or didn't want to be found. Little evidence, no one wanting to talk. And here, not knowing what police agency should investigate.

"Have you contacted the Bureau of Indian Affairs or the FBI?" Kelly asked. The seminar had taught her that much.

Sweka's face tensed. "I reported Therese's concerns to the BIA, but I haven't heard back."

Kelly remembered the seminar talking about how seldom the BIA and FBI became involved in missing Indigenous person cases. And how the jurisdictional maze of law enforcement and prosecution made it simpler to assume it was someone else's problem. Kelly knew if her daughter were missing, she'd be raging, demanding attention, not nearly as calm as Therese.

"Is she living with someone who could have hurt her?" Kelly asked. A history of domestic violence should get somebody's attention.

Therese shrugged. "Tyler never seemed violent to me. They argued, but she never told me he hit her."

"We have resources at my office if you find out there has been," Kelly said. She felt around in her suit jacket pocket and pulled out business cards that she handed to Sweka and Therese.

"Will you help me?" Therese asked again, this time looking directly at Kelly.

Kelly flinched, feeling guilty she wanted to put off this sad woman. Obligations already overwhelmed her. "I'm sorry, but missing persons are a police matter, and right now I need to get back. Be sure to file a report with the sheriff's office, OK?"

Therese's shoulders slumped as she nodded.

IN THE SILENCE of the drive back, Kelly's stomach clenched, and her thoughts raced. Someone needed to help Therese find her daughter. Why wasn't the BIA taking more of an interest? What was the matter with the City of Galmenberg? Their inattention pricked her anger and resentment. Do I really need to get involved? Years of parochial schools and homilies about the Good Samaritan and bearing each other's burdens made Kelly's body heavy and weak. *I need to spend more time with Ruth.* She pushed thoughts of Therese out of her head. *I'm already away too much with this job that never lets up.*

Kelly forced herself to concentrate on this afternoon's hearing as she opened her office door. She was waking up her computer when Carmen loomed in the doorway.

"I'm starting to dread seeing you," Kelly said.

"I know. I'm sorry. I'm just the messenger," Carmen said.

"What now?"

"The boss wants to hold a public event, make us more visible, and wants you to organize it. You can pick two others to help you."

Kelly groaned inside. Organizing a program took time, energy, and interest she didn't have. "Another one? Does he remember I'm already part of next week's community event?"

Carmen raised her shoulders and gave Kelly a pitying smile. "I guess it comes with being a senior deputy. He said you could delegate if you preferred. And it doesn't need to happen until October."

"OK." Kelly twirled her gavel pencil, a souvenir from the trip she took with Ruth to the Supreme Court last summer. Its hopeful inscription, *With liberty and justice for all,* seemed ironic today. Prosecuting Attorney Richard Paltik was an elected official. And a good boss. A lot better than her supervisor in Seattle. She'd ask Clara and Dave when they met about the community event in a few minutes. Dave was the youngest attorney in the office, two years out of law school, and always eager to share his opinions. Clara and Kelly had worked together for many years now, and Kelly relied on her political smarts.

Dave and Clara arrived together at Kelly's office promptly at eleven-thirty. Dave's short sleeved shirt revealed a glimpse of a colorful geometric tat as he held the door for Clara. He wasn't wearing a tie, and Kelly wondered whether he didn't think he had anything important to do today. Dave was like many of the younger attorneys she'd seen at bar association meetings lately—casually dressed, long hair pulled into a low ponytail, sometimes an ear cuff. She had to get used to it. Clara was older, nearly Kelly's age, and wore a beige linen suit with a high-necked blouse.

Dave looked quizzical, then irritated when Kelly explained the proposed October session.

"Don't worry, I'll ask for other volunteers," Kelly said. "I was just hoping you could help me brainstorm. We're ready for the next week's presentation unless you have concerns."

Dave shook his head. "I figured this would be a short meeting, though."

Kelly recognized the frazzled I-have-too-much-to-do-for-this tone of his voice.

"I think we're good," Clara said.

"You should do something controversial if you want people to come," Dave said.

"How about something related to all the missing Indigenous women?" Kelly said. "I could set the date for Indigenous People's Day formerly known as Columbus Day."

Dave scrunched his face, jutting out his chin and furrowing his brow. "That seems more like a resource issue than a legal one."

"A pay-attention-and-do-something issue," Clara said. "But not in our wheelhouse."

"We could do privacy and DNA testing," Dave said. "Cases where police used those genealogy services are working their way through the courts. Or police use of facial recognition software. You could invite somebody from ACLU or the defense bar to counter the state's position."

Kelly kept her hands hidden underneath the desk as she ravaged her cuticles. The muscles in the back of her neck tightened, and she pushed up her glasses. "I was thinking something helpful to the average person. And since we're focusing on county regulations next week, maybe this one should focus on something less . . . arcane."

"You know, whatever we do, people will just use it as a forum to complain. I know Paltik wants these sessions to be informational and as apolitical as possible, but that's the truth. And privacy is important to everybody. Just because we represent law enforcement doesn't mean we're blind to the constitutional issues," Dave said. "We're about justice here, aren't we?"

Justice. Kelly had always thought that was the side she was on. But sometimes it felt cloudy, dark, inconclusive. The big databases frightened her, and she was suspicious of those genealogy sites that collected DNA for who knows what purposes. Should everybody in a family be a suspect because of one bad third-cousin once removed? But she wanted killers off the streets, too.

"OK, thanks," Kelly said. "We've got thirty minutes to figure out the schedule and what we still need for next week. The boss will talk first, of course, but then what?"

Dave tore a handwritten sheet from his yellow pad. "I worked one up. What do you think?"

As she and Clara scanned Dave's notes, Kelly didn't know whether to be grateful or irritated at Dave's preempting discussion with his proposal, but the sequence would work and she decided she didn't care enough to quarrel. "Clara?"

"Looks good to me." Clara shrugged.

"OK. Thanks Dave," Kelly said.

"Lunch?" Clara asked once Dave fled the room.

"I brought mine. And I have a hearing this afternoon," Kelly said.

"I've got a box in the freezer," Clara said.

"OK. But only a half hour."

Kelly followed Clara to the break room and pulled her own microwave meal out of the freezer.

"How's Ruthy?" Clara asked as they took turns waiting for the microwave.

"The same. Sometimes it feels like one night elves substituted a changeling for my sweet, beautiful child."

"Don't all parents of teenagers think that? And what about those terrible twos?"

"Ruth didn't go through that. She was very quiet at first. I was always so proud of what a great mother I must be when the day care workers would say how well-behaved she was. Until now." Kelly wondered if abandonment fears kept the young Ruth quiet and compliant, fears the foster agency said all foster and adopted kids had and showed in different ways.

"You are a great mother," Clara said as they pushed aside papers to clear a space on the small round table in Kelly's office.

"I don't know," Kelly said. "I'm gone a lot. Distracted when I'm home. At least my mom was around when I got home after school."

"C'mon. You wouldn't wish your childhood on Ruthy."

True, she wouldn't. Despite having lost her faith years ago, the guilt and fear of her upbringing haunted her. She wondered what would haunt Ruth years from now. Everyone has something.

Kelly ate quickly. "I need to prepare," she said, and Clara rose. "Why don't you come over to the house sometime and have a glass of wine? Or we could organize a happy hour?"

"Good idea," Clara said as she left.

After reading through the file, Kelly drove to the courthouse as she'd cut it too short to walk the half mile in spike heels. She waved to the parking attendant checking juror passes. The courthouse complex was relatively new and convenient, but she was glad her office remained in the elegant red stone building of the old one. All this concrete and glass just didn't give the same sense of weightiness as the old spires and nooks and columns. Kelly remembered the political firestorm when the sheriff's department needed more room. Years of failed bond elections forced the county to rent space in old vacant buildings across the city, and the expense of that was borne by cuts in other departments. When a scaled down version finally passed, the old courthouse's neighbors didn't want to sell, and the county commissioners built this complex down the street, then fixed up the old courthouse into offices for themselves, county administration, and the prosecuting attorney's office. The judges grumbled, but Kelly supposed it made sense to build holding cells below the courtrooms and house the sheriff's office in this cold monstrosity. Efficient instead of charming.

Kelly passed Sheriff Nisser standing tall and straight in his crisp dress uniform near the courtrooms.

"I hear you were at our crime scene this morning, counselor," he said. "What did you think? Pretty sure Springer thought I'd sent him on a fool's errand."

"Only time will tell," Kelly said, rushing into the courtroom when she saw defense counsel enter.

THREE HUGE FLAGS in front of the building snapped in the wind, and an untethered rope clanged against the flagpole, sounding like a buoy in a summer squall as Kelly pulled out of the garage after the hearing. The darkening sky threatened another big storm, and Kelly twitched with anxiety. She needed to make sure Ruth was all right, home safe. The rain intensified as she drove, and thoughts of the missing girl alone or worse in this wild weather tumbled with her fears about Ruth, adding to the familiar panic that started the day she first left Ruth at the daycare. Fear was a big part of her being a mom, part guilt over her many hours away and a nagging sense that no matter what she did, it was never enough.

Kelly feared it was her fault Ruth was so prickly, so antagonistic, so willing to ascribe the worst motives to whatever Kelly said or did. Feared their endless conflicts about homework and boys and curfews and clothing would drive Ruth to rebel in stupid ways, maybe even run away. Is that what happened to the missing girl? She ran away and couldn't get back?

It had to change. Kelly couldn't bear the thought of Ruth missing. They needed to be kinder to each other.

"Anybody home?" Kelly yelled as she unlocked the door between the garage and the house.

But the house was dark and cold and silent except for the quick flap of Babs coming in through the kitty door. Babs stood in the kitchen and meowed until Kelly filled her bowl with kibble and the fishy wet food that made it palatable to the spoiled cat.

"Where's Ruthy?" Kelly asked, but Babs was too busy to answer.

Kelly peered into the darkening yard with its fraying lawn chairs placed haphazardly on the patchy grass, then checked her messages and the calendar hanging on the refrigerator. She wracked her brain trying to remember if there was anything going on, any place Ruth might expect her to be. Finally, she called, no response, then texted.

"Home soon. Chill," Ruth texted back.

A wave of relief flowed through Kelly. "Want to go out for supper tonight?"

"No."

"Do you have an ETA? Where are you?"

"20."

"OK."

Kelly changed into loose navy sweatpants, their elastic waist a relief after spending all day in shaping pantyhose. She wanted to lose weight, but who had time to go to the gym or scour the internet for, and experiment with, low-cal recipes? She refused to try those meal plan services that promised great taste and good health. That was admitting defeat. She hung her suit on the door and threw her blouse in the laundry before removing her bra and putting on a loose T-shirt. She found fuzzy socks near the bed. She preferred bare feet, but the tile in the kitchen was still cold in the evenings.

As Kelly browned onions and peppers on the stove and breathed in their comforting smell, a familiar exhaustion crept over her. Why did it have to be so hard? She'd read enough books and articles to know the teenage years were difficult. Hell, she'd rebelled against her parents' rules, justified as religious precepts, too. But she longed for a little respect, a little affection. Ruth assumed every question was a criticism, every suggestion a reproof.

Ruth came into the kitchen with a thud of dropped books and backpack, and she unlaced, then kicked off her Doc Martens. A small, dirty puddle formed as she shook off the rain and hung her hoodie over the nearest chair. She tucked a strand of blue and black hair behind her ears and looked at Kelly accusingly, of what, Kelly had no idea.

"Want some spaghetti?" Kelly said, straining pasta over the sink.

Ruth nodded.

"Should I brown meat or do you just want marinara sauce?"

"Mom, you know I'm a vegetarian."

Kelly filled a cereal bowl with noodles, ladled red sauce on top, then put the bowl on the kitchen table. *This week she's a vegetarian, but last month she wanted steaks on the grill. Who can keep up?* She dumped a bag of premixed salad into a bowl and set out a tub of grated parmesan.

"Is that vegan cheese?" Ruth asked.

"No," Kelly said. She drew the line at fake cheese. "But no animals died in its production."

"Not the only issue, Mom," Ruth said, but sprinkled cheese on her pasta before turning back to her phone.

"How was your day?" Kelly asked to break the silence.

"Good," Ruth said, scrolling through her phone as she ate.

"Want to Skype grandma tonight?"

Ruth had a soft spot for Grandma, was more generous in her affection than Kelly found herself able to be. Kelly was dutiful, calling weekly and visiting once a year, but the unspoken formed a wall that had only hardened over the years. Having Ruth on the call lessened the tension, and her mom smiled more.

Ruth lowered her phone. "Aren't we going to call on Sunday?"

"We can. But I thought we should start planning our trip to Chicago."

"I've got plans tonight." Ruth went back to her phone.

"What plans?"

Ruth gave Kelly a withering look. "Emily's house. We're finishing our final project."

"During exam week?"

"It's due on Wednesday, so yes, time's tight."

"What's the project? Anything I can help with?"

"Global warming," Ruth said without looking up. "And no."

Kelly didn't want to give up on conversation that easily, but the minutes dragged on as she tried to figure out what might interest Ruth. "I met a woman today whose daughter is missing."

No response.

"We could post flyers for her. Can you think of any place to put them?"

"Not really."

Kelly stifled her irritation. *What about the high school? What about showing your friends? Posting on your social media? What about offering to take some and asking around? Do you have no social conscience at all?*

Ruth got up, rinsed her bowl, put it next to the sink, and left the kitchen. A few minutes later, the front door slammed.

How hard is it to put it in the dishwasher?

TWO

TUESDAY

A STACCATO RAIN provided a rhythm for Kelly's frenetic morning routine. Get up. Take a shower. Knock on Ruth's door. Put on her blue suit. Find her pair of navy heels. Tell Ruth to get up. Go downstairs. Make coffee. Pour cereal. Yell the time up the stairs. Climb the stairs. Find Ruth still in bed, cocooned in her quilt with her pillow covering her head.

"Get up," Kelly said from the doorway to Ruth's room, having previously been banned from entering without permission. "If you'd go to bed on time, getting up wouldn't be so hard."

"I had to finish my homework, like you always tell me," Ruth said as she slid her feet to the floor and stood. "It's exam week, you know." She kicked a pile of loose clothes next to the bed and bumped Kelly's shoulder as she passed.

Do all families go through this every morning, or is it just us? Kelly wondered as she hurried down the stairs.

"What do you want on your bagel?" Kelly shouted up the stairs.

"Can't we do the drive-through?" Ruth yelled from behind the closed bathroom door.

"No time," Kelly said.

"Peanut butter on one side, cream cheese on the other."

Well, at least she'll get some protein. Kelly peered through the sliding glass door at the covered patio where Babs stalked unseen prey and toward the wet lawn that needed mowing. Pockets of fog shrouded nearby trees.

Ruth rumbled down the stairs and zipped up her black hoodie. Kelly only glimpsed the white of a graphic T-shirt underneath. The school had rules about those, and she guessed Ruth was testing those limits, too. *Their problem,* she decided, knowing the school would be unlikely to do anything during this last week of classes before summer break. Ruth slung her backpack over one shoulder, then grabbed the bagel off the counter. Kelly'd long ago given up making lunches in favor of subscribing to the high school's meal plan. More choices for Ruth, easier mornings for Kelly. It was hard enough to get Ruth to eat breakfast.

Ruth ate in the car, staring at her phone the entire drive. She pulled her hood over her blue-tipped black hair and slammed the car door without saying goodbye when they arrived. Kelly felt both guilt and relief as Ruth ran toward the school's massive double doors, lost in a sea of teenagers also wearing shapeless black hoodies and baggy black pants. The car behind her beeped, reminding her to get going.

Even the triple-shot latte Kelly bought from the drive-through on her way to the office didn't give her the energy to leave her car. She tried not to resent Ruth's dawdling that often made Kelly the last one to arrive at the Cascadia County Prosecuting Attorney's Office, no matter how early she set her alarm. She stared through the rain at the employee entrance, then chugged the last of her coffee, gathered the folders strewn next to her purse, pulled her coat's hood up, and left the warmth of her car for the pungent wet of the parking lot. She ran through the downpour toward the back entrance.

Once inside, Kelly let her hood drop and raked her fingers through her limp hair, glad she didn't spend much time on it this morning. She hoped she didn't look too much a fright. Opposing counsel once told her she reminded him of Janet Reno. Kelly was sure that was a not-so-subtle dig at her short haircut, intense manner, and boxy suits. Kelly said thank you anyway.

"Another fine day," Kelly said to Dave as he walked past carrying a Sierra Club mug full to the brim with black coffee.

"We're living the dream," Dave said without stopping.

Kelly hung her wet coat on the back of her office door, threw her purse on her chair, wiped the fog off her glasses with a tissue, and headed toward the lobby. Today was her morning as Attorney-of-the-Day, a program instituted by Paltik, who had promised during his campaign to make his office more accessible. Many of the attorneys complained, said it was paralegal work since they couldn't give legal advice to anyone but clients, but Kelly liked the chance to talk with regular people instead of just bureaucrats and lawyers and judges. Inefficient, but real.

She grabbed a pile of messages from her box behind Carmen's desk. People hate talking to voice mail, Carmen often complained. *Then what's the point of our fancy-dancy voice to email program?* Kelly often thought. It made more sense to use that money to hire another lawyer. The computer techs did not agree, promised big savings on staff time and salary costs.

Sure.

Kelly picked up the clipboard holding the sign-in sheet for walk-ins. Despite the fact they held no appointments before nine, several people waited on the plastic chairs in front of the reception desk. She recognized Therese sitting near the back, wearing a colorful long skirt and embroidered poncho, her hands grasping an umbrella in her lap, her eyes closed. Hers was the first name on the clipboard.

"Therese?" Kelly asked.

Therese looked up.

"Good to see you again. Hope the rain didn't make it too hard to get here," Kelly said.

Therese stood, pain showing in the line of her mouth and sadness in her eyes. "Bus only runs in the rez once every two hours, but they let us wait in the Casino."

"You can follow me if you don't mind waiting while I get organized."

Therese followed Kelly through the narrow hallway toward her windowless office. As the number of staff grew, the size of their office space hadn't, and visitors needed an escort to find anyone.

"Coffee? Water?" Kelly asked as she motioned for Therese to sit in the chair in front of the desk.

Therese shook her head.

Kelly sat in the big blue roller chair behind her desk and picked up a lined yellow pad. "You told me yesterday your daughter was missing. Is that why you're here?"

Therese nodded.

"Like I said yesterday," Kelly said as gently as she could, "the police handle missing persons cases, not this office."

A spark of anger and frustration flashed over Therese's face, then a stubbornness.

"I've tried. Everybody says it's somebody else's problem. Daniel told me the prosecuting attorney had a program where we could just ask questions. That's why I came." Therese looked away, and her shoulders fell. "I didn't know I'd be talking to you again."

A wave of guilt washed over Kelly. "You're right. You can ask anything, and I'll answer as best I can."

"Who will help me?" Therese asked. "There must be someone who will."

Kelly sat back in her chair. She did not know the answer. All she knew was that Therese's problems navigating the complex system of cross-jurisdictional crime was common. And here, no one even knew if there had been a crime. She turned to the bookcase where she kept her seminar materials and pawed through a messy file. She pulled out a yellow folder stuffed with loose paper and skimmed a list of resources.

"Therese, a couple of agencies deal with missing women. I'll give you a copy of this list. Have you filed a report with the sheriff?"

"Not yet."

"Let's do that too." Kelly typed on her keyboard and pulled up a copy of the sheriff's form on her computer screen. "Let's start at the beginning. Why do you think your daughter is missing?"

"Dee called me, asked for money I didn't have."

"That was the last time you talked with her?"

"Yeah."

"When was that?" Kelly nodded as she typed.

"Three weeks ago. I felt bad. Called her several times over the next week, but she never answered. I figured she was giving me the silent treatment, so I even left her a message that I could give her some money. She always calls back when I say that. I called my cousin in Galmenberg, said to go check on her. Nobody answered the door for him or for me two days later." Therese swept a tear from her cheek.

Kelly clenched her hands as she listened.

"I told Daniel. He's the officer you met yesterday. Tribal police look every day on their rounds for abandoned cars, and . . ." Therese hesitated, and Kelly could guess what Therese was picturing in her head. Therese caught her breath and covered her face with her hands. "My cousin Layla put up posters at the Casino and my neighbors' kids put some up in the schools. I've put up posters where I could, although most shops in Galmenberg say no and the ones on poles keep getting torn down. I called the hospital. Called her friends. Had my cousin drive me around the neighborhood again. Tried to talk to her boyfriend, but he didn't answer. Daniel said I needed to file a report with Galmenberg police so I did. I don't know what else to do."

"Did you give the Galmenberg police a picture?" Kelly said in her most soothing voice.

Therese nodded.

Kelly pushed up her glasses. She felt as helpless as Therese. She knew Therese was just trying to find someone who would listen, would do something. "What did they say?"

"That she's an adult and leaving her boyfriend isn't a crime."

Not helpful, but not wrong.

Therese pulled out a sheaf of papers from her woven straw bag and handed it to Kelly. On it was a large picture of a pretty young woman with the word

MISSING: DEE (DIYANNI) HUPT in large letters. "Here are posters my cousin Layla made. Hand them around. Anywhere, to anyone. Please."

A typical high school senior picture. Her long dark hair framed a round face then dropped to the bottom of the frame. She had a mischievous grin, but somber eyes and a small crease between her eyebrows. A beauty who'd grown up too fast. She wore a blue scooped top and around her neck a brightly colored carved orca on a beaded chain.

"You have a daughter," Therese said, pointing to a framed picture on Kelly's desk. "How old?"

"Fourteen."

Therese sighed. "A hard age."

"Indeed," Kelly said. "Do you know if the police contacted anyone?"

Therese folded her arms. "They don't tell me nothing. Say I have to be patient. Say she'll come home."

"Who said that?"

"Officer Fisher in Galmenberg."

"I went to a seminar that talked about a missing persons database. Let's make sure Diyanni is on that list if she isn't already. OK?"

Therese nodded, tears forming in the corners of her eyes.

"Everybody's going to want to have the basic information, so let's fill out this missing persons form together and get it to the sheriff. They'll want to know things like where she lived and worked, when you or anyone last saw her, any other names she used, and who her boyfriend was."

"I told Officer Fisher all that."

"Tell me."

For the next half hour Kelly pried, and Therese hesitated at each question. Diyanni had moved to Galmenberg with her boyfriend, Tyler, right after high school. Tyler was bad news according to Therese's description. Diyanni said she was a waitress, but never told Therese which restaurant. Therese knew Diyanni drank, feared she may have started using drugs since she moved in with Tyler. The last time Therese had seen Tyler his pupils were tiny, and he was constantly scratching his arms.

"Do you have an email address?"

"No. I don't have a computer," Therese said.

"You probably should set one up using one of the library's or a community center's computer so people can contact you."

"OK," Therese said, but Kelly could see from Therese's hesitation that the thought upset her.

"A librarian or staff member can help you set it up," Kelly said.

Therese nodded.

"Read through this form then bring it to the sheriff's office," Kelly said as she pulled several pages from her printer and handed them to Therese. "I'll show you how to get there when I walk you out. They'll want you to sign an affidavit. Now let's put a little pressure on Officer Fisher. See what he's done." Kelly searched online for the number of the Galmenberg City Police Department and called.

Kelly could hear the irritation in Fisher's voice from his first word.

"What's been done so far?" Kelly asked. "Have you sent the report to State Patrol? Got her on the Missing Persons database?"

"I'm doing my job," Fisher said. "She's an adult and the guy she lives with hasn't reported her missing. We don't know there's been a crime. And it hasn't been thirty days yet."

Fisher's tone made Kelly sit up straighter. "I'll make a records request for her file if you prefer."

"You know you can't get information on an ongoing investigation," Fisher said.

"Oh, I think your city attorney's office will give it to me, and besides Ms. Hupt can."

"Listen," Officer Fisher said in a tone bristling with condescension. "We sent a patrol officer to her house, and her boyfriend isn't worried. Said she was headed to the rez the last time he saw her. I called the BIA and the FBI, and neither of them had the decency to call me back. Indians go missing all the time, but do they follow up? No. They want us to do their work. Well, we're busy too. And have a lot less funding."

"She lives in Galmenberg," Kelly said, not wanting to argue with him with Therese listening. "That's your jurisdiction."

The clatter of sliding chairs and hushed conversation filled the telephone line. "Mrs. Hupt is welcome to come in again and we'll talk."

"Tomorrow?"

"Thursday. One o'clock." Then silence.

Kelly didn't know what bothered her most, the unrelenting layers of bureaucracy and procedures or his obvious disrespect. Sometimes life seemed a constant resistance. Confronting belligerent opposing counsel refusing to explain a child's injuries. Outmaneuvering condescending lawyers who thought public lawyers were stupid and lazy. Defying the guys in law school who thought women shouldn't be lawyers, and coworkers who thought the same thing. Kelly damn well wouldn't let it get the better of her or let anyone see. If anything, it made her more resolute.

"He says you should come in Thursday," Kelly said.

Therese nodded, resignation and defeat evident in the slope of her body.

"Will you come with me?" Therese asked.

Kelly hesitated. She was busy. Had too much to do. If she took time off, she should spend it with Ruth. But her trial had been postponed. She could go.

"The police will listen to you better than an Indian," Therese said.

Kelly thought that was true. Her years of being a lawyer had given her a steel most people didn't have. And most people found "unladylike." Too bad. A wave of guilt clutched at her gut. She knew she was lucky in ways she didn't deserve, she had parents who sent her to college, gave her money when she was struggling. She needed to give time as well as money. Maybe she could even talk Paltik into seeing it as part of her job.

"OK. And we could try to find Tyler ahead of time." Kelly looked at her appointment schedule. "Can you meet me here around ten on Thursday?"

Therese brightened, picked up her umbrella, and stood. "Thank you."

"It's hard for you to get here, isn't it," Kelly said.

"It's fine."

"Tell you what, I'll pick you up. It will give us more time to talk."

Therese gave Kelly a grateful smile as she drew a map with directions to her house. It was farther out than Kelly had hoped, but she'd already offered. Kelly walked Therese to the front of the courthouse and pointed down the street, glad the rain had cleared to a light mist. "Go five blocks to a newer cement and glass building. It will have a big sign. The sheriff's office entrance is next to the parking garage. You can't miss it."

Therese nodded and clutched the papers as she walked away.

KELLY POSTED THE MISSING flyer on the board in the break room and decided not to involve Paltik just yet. *Don't get personally involved,* he would say. But how could she not? She took a coffee to her desk to write a quick contact summary. She picked up Ruth's baby picture from her desk, remembering the day she first saw her.

Kelly had been at the county's social services office to meet with the department head about an angry parent's claim her child had been taken without good cause. *How hard this job must be, trying to decide if a parent is a danger to a child,* she'd thought as she passed a social worker's office. The social worker was on the phone, and in a carrier on the floor sat a silent baby who looked at Kelly with somber wide eyes that pierced Kelly's soul somehow. The department head explained they were trying to place the abandoned girl. A shop owner found the baby on a sidewalk, skinny, whimpering, and sitting in a filthy diaper made from an old T-shirt, next to a woman overdosed on heroin. At the hospital, the recovering woman asked for her baby once, but disappeared shortly after her release. Kelly's heart broke when she heard they were struggling to find a home for the baby as most foster homes were already filled and many potential adopters balked at the idea of a dark-skinned baby who likely had neonatal abstinence syndrome. Kelly offered to foster the baby for the weekend. A relieved social worker told Kelly what she needed to get, and after a quick home inspection dropped the baby off.

By the end of the weekend, Kelly couldn't let her go back, got her mom to fly out from Chicago to help as Kelly negotiated parental leave, and after ten months of investigations, doctors' appointments, motions, arguments, hearings, court orders, and delays, she adopted Ruth on what they celebrated as Ruth's birthday. She didn't regret getting involved then, or even now that their relationship was so strained. Ruth had no memory of her birth mother and no way to find her, but since Ruth became a teenager she'd begun including "You're not my mom," among the many taunts and accusations she threw at Kelly. *This will pass,* Kelly told herself.

Kelly went to the front and called the next name on Carmen's list.

KELLY WAS HUNGRY to the point of shaking after her last walk-in. The nearest drive-through would have to do. She needed to figure out how to get Paltik's authorization to spend her time and county resources on figuring out what happened to Therese's daughter. Had to be something practical as Kelly had heard him say more than once that castles in the air were for undergraduates and lawyers needed to concentrate on the possible.

As Kelly drove, she noticed all the political signs littering the streets and blocking her view when she wanted to turn right. Large ones for the federal candidates demanded *CHANGE IN 2014,* and often blocked the small ones that had only a face and a name for the local races. Paltik's pale, handsome face leaped out from a prominent red and blue one on a busy corner: *Justice For All. Reelect Richard Paltik for Cascadia County Prosecuting Attorney.* The election. That had to be the way in.

Paltik's office light was on when Kelly got back, having finished her chicken sandwich with fries and a chocolate shake, comfort food for an uncomfortable morning, in a parking lot near the bay. Resolute, she knocked on his door as he stared at his computer screen, his hand buried in his sandy blond hair and his tie and black rimmed glasses slightly askew. A panoramic view of the city and the mountains to the east filled the wall of windows behind him. He smiled and waved her in.

"What's up?" he said.

"I was at Galmenberg Bay yesterday, where they found that shoe," she began.

He laughed. "Is the county or the Nininpak Police taking the case?"

"The county. What's interesting is that one of the women who found it was afraid it was her missing daughter's."

Paltik sat up straight and frowned. He'd been at the missing women seminar too, and his interest encouraged Kelly. "Was it?"

"Deputy Springer doesn't think so, but I got the impression the mom thinks no one is looking too hard for her daughter. She came in for attorney-of-the-day this morning."

"And you think we should help her," Paltik said, crossing his arms and creasing his stiff blue shirt.

"You know how hard it is for people to maneuver through the various systems. I got the sense the Nininpak Nation isn't getting much cooperation. I'm not saying we should take on the full investigation. It'd be constituent service."

Paltik looked at Kelly over the top of his glasses and gave her a wry smile. "You want me to think this will help with the tribal vote."

"It can't hurt. But I'll help her out on my own time if that seems better."

"A little pro bono work is fine unless conflicts turn up, or it takes up a lot of time. Keep me informed." Paltik adjusted his glasses and returned to his screen and pulling at his hair.

Relieved and hopeful, Kelly was thankful yet again for her job with this county attorney. When she graduated from law school, she'd joined a big law firm that promised to support her pro bono aspirations while paying a salary sizable enough to help her pay off her student loans. She wanted to make a difference, help people, but she needed to be practical too. Her disillusionment started when her billable hours were criticized at her six-month review, despite her being at the office ten hours a day. She started working weekends, but knew she wasn't keeping up with the other associates and didn't know what to change. She had no time or energy to do her laundry or cook, let alone volunteer. She envied the married men with their wives taking care of all the things at home and not seeming to need or want any other social life.

She'd ignored the guys at law school who'd complained about her and other women who'd taken spots from men and was surprised to find out some had similar thoughts at the law firm, as if women didn't support themselves and their families too. After two years, Kelly knew she needed to move on and joined the Seattle Division of the Attorney General's Office. Yes, she worked a lot of hours and plenty of her coworkers and client departments underestimated her, but at least she didn't have those damned billable hours. She developed thick skin, but knew it had its personal cost. It had been years since she had a romantic partner for more than a few weeks. And she had to leave when she was turned down, again, for a promotion she was sure had been rigged from the start.

Back in her office, Kelly read an email from Deputy Springer, surprised and irritated that he was the lead in Diyanni's case. *Not important enough for the Missing Persons Unit Detective?*

"We're going to try to find the boyfriend on Thursday, see when he saw her last," she told Springer when she called him. "Do you know if there are any similar cases?"

"I haven't looked yet," he said.

"Anything new on the shoe?" Kelly asked.

"Not much. Dr. Green says she's ninety-nine percent sure it's a man's bone and there's remodeling from prior injuries. DNA will take a while as this one's a low priority so long as there's no suspicion of murder."

"So, not the girl, anyway," Kelly said.

"Looks like not."

THREE

WEDNESDAY

DETECTIVE CONNOR ANDINO looked out his office window past the grimy streets out toward the sliver of Galmenberg Bay he could just make out at the edge of the horizon. He swiveled toward the door when he heard a quick knock and throat clearing. The sheriff had a slim file folder in his hand.

"We've got a new missing person's case," the sheriff said. "A Nininpak woman. The prosecuting attorney's office has gotten involved, so you should probably get up to speed with what we have."

Connor opened the file. All it held was an initial report and notes from a Deputy Springer. "Is Springer working on this?"

"He can help you if you need it, but I want you to liaise with the attorneys. Springer can be a little . . . unpolitic."

"Will do," Connor said as the sheriff left.

As the head, and only member, of Cascadia County's new Missing Persons' Unit, Connor knew Indigenous women went missing more, and were found less often, than other missing persons. It had been true when he'd worked in Las Vegas, too. He didn't know why, but the perception was that the police worked harder to find white women. He hoped that wasn't true, suspected it probably was, and promised himself he'd treat everyone the same.

The notes were scanty, and Connor winced when he saw the last time anyone reported seeing Diyanni was a couple of weeks ago at a party on the Reservation. The first two to three days of a case were the most important. Every day it got harder for anyone to remember anything, and the chances for any physical evidence were small. *No one knows if she left or is missing.* But if she were, finding her got more difficult by the day.

Connor went to find Springer. The open area of the office was noisy with ringing telephones and deputies talking on the phone or shouting across the room at each other. Springer's desk was close to the main entrance. Connor found Springer scrutinizing a picture of a black shoe on his phone. Several similar shoes filled his desktop's screen.

"Deputy Springer?" Connor said, and Springer looked up, startled. "I understand you know something about this missing woman?"

Springer glanced at the notes in the folder Connor held out. "Not much more than I said in those notes. I was at the beach for a floating foot." He showed Connor his phone, and Connor could now see water and seaweed surrounding the shoe. "One of the women asked if it could be her daughter. The answer is no. I guess the mom went to the county attorney's office yesterday, met with the attorney who was at the scene too."

"Which attorney?"

"Kelly Flynn. I'd never met her before that."

"I haven't either. I'll call her. Anything on the foot?"

"Pretty sure it's this one." Springer pointed to an all-black shoe with a distinctive sole in the center of his computer screen. "Not too helpful, though. It was mass produced for the last six years with thousands sold in Washington and Canada. We're not going to identify the bones this way, but at least we know it couldn't have entered the sea more than six years ago."

"Interesting," Connor said. No, there'd never been anything like that in Las Vegas, although he'd heard about several since he moved to the Pacific Northwest. "Good luck."

"Thanks," Springer said. "And if you need anything on the missing person's case, let me know."

What next? Connor went back through the maze of cubicles to his office. One person had seen the girl at the Casino on the rez on Memorial Day, she lived in Galmenberg. How was this a county case? It wasn't, he decided, but he'd promised the sheriff he'd look into it. No one answered the phone at the local Bureau of Indian Affairs Office, so he left a message.

Maybe Ms. Flynn could give him a lead. He sat back in his chair as the phone rang, this time looking at the old red brick building down the street he knew held the prosecuting attorney's office.

"Thanks for getting back to me so quickly," Kelly said when Connor was finally connected. "Yes, I talked with Therese Hupt yesterday. I have a hearing in a half hour at the courthouse. Should I come up after?"

"Sure. If your hearing goes long, we could talk over lunch?"

"Perfect. See you then."

Just after eleven, Connor heard a woman with a loud, deep voice asking a sergeant at the counter where his office might be. He stood in his doorway and motioned to the sergeant to let her pass. Connor guessed she was about forty. She wore a navy business suit with a soft powder blue shirt that tied with a bow at her neck. Her chin length hair was mussed in the way of someone who had combed it with her hands without looking at a mirror. As she walked toward him she pushed up her blue plastic glasses and extended her hand.

"Detective Andino?" she asked.

Connor nodded and shook her hand. Her hand was warm, her grip tentative.

"I'm Kelly Flynn. Thanks for making time for me."

Connor couldn't help but appreciate a lawyer who thanked him for his time. In his experience, lawyers were usually too busy for cops. Unless they wanted something. *She probably wants something.*

"We can talk here, or over lunch. Whatever you prefer," Connor said.

"Let's talk about Therese here to keep her confidentiality," Kelly said. "But I'll need lunch too if you have time after."

For the next ten minutes Kelly recounted the meeting at the beach, told Connor her impressions of Therese, and complained about how the Galmenberg police seemed unresponsive. As far as Kelly knew, no one had talked to Dee's boyfriend or coworkers and she was hoping to do that tomorrow as well as try to pressure Galmenberg into being more proactive. Connor could see Kelly was worked up. He wondered why.

"Thanks," Connor said when she finished. "This is all good information that's hard to put in a written report. I'm wondering, though, what's your role here. The prosecuting attorney's office doesn't usually get involved until, well, there's a crime to prosecute. Doesn't seem like we're there yet."

Kelly sat back in her chair and looked at him intently. "I know. My boss asked the same thing." She leaned closer, put her elbows on his desk. "But it's important, and I know how hard it is for the average person, let alone someone living on the rez, to navigate the legal system. When I met Therese on the beach on Monday she seemed bewildered about what to do as well as worried about her daughter. My heart went out to her."

"You're a softy, then," Connor said, smiling.

"I have a teenage daughter. The thought of her going missing is one of my worst fears. How can I not help?"

Connor nodded. "We'll do what we can here, but you know about the jurisdictional issues."

"I do. It's why I was called out to the beach in the first place. I wish there were a cross-jurisdictional task force to deal with these issues."

"There should be. And if there isn't we should create one."

"I agree," Kelly said, a broad smile brightening her face before collapsing into a frown. "I'd be afraid, I'm sure Therese is afraid, Diyanni's been abducted or worse."

Connor sat back in his chair. "That's every parent's fear, but until we have some evidence it's hard to tell whether someone's just decided to disappear. I worked Missing Persons in Las Vegas before coming here."

Kelly leaned forward and tilted her head as if asking for more.

"Lots of missing persons, strippers, sex workers, gay men, kids on vacation. A lot of them were escaping some pretty bad situations."

"Native women?" Kelly asked.

"Sure, lots of reservations nearby. And while it's true traffickers and serial killers prey on marginalized people, it's also true that many people hide from the bad situations they've just left."

Kelly nodded, her forehead wrinkled.

"I can't say this to the media, and I won't say it to the parents, but how do you tell the difference? And don't tell me to treat all missing persons cases with the same intensity as a child abduction. We don't have the resources. I'm just one guy. Galmenberg's missing persons unit is just one guy. We have to prioritize. You may as well know, the biggest reason I'm spending time on this case is because you took an interest and the sheriff wants to play nice with the prosecutor's office. Is that fair to the other cases?"

Kelly shook her head.

"No, it isn't. And sometimes the media takes an interest and we reshuffle our priorities again." Connor crossed his arms.

"So, what are the priorities if I hadn't shown up?"

"Missing children get first priority and AMBER alerts. Vulnerable persons who are unlikely to have left on their own or may have trouble finding their way home, like seniors and the disabled, people from assisted living homes. Adults who are in domestic violence or other threatening situations get priority over someone who hasn't called their mom for a few weeks."

Kelly flinched and sighed. "What do you tell a mom whose daughter hasn't called for a few weeks?"

"We take the report. Put it on the missing persons database. Tell the mom to keep calling her and talk to her friends, her employer, and get back to us if she gets any leads or in a week."

"A week? What if it's already been several weeks?"

"Then it depends on if there are other red flags, like missed appointments or a conscientious employee not turning up for work. And if there are other priority cases or staffing issues."

"I'm sorry if it seems like I'm hassling you. We have workload issues, too. And not every case gets the same attention as a death penalty trial or bank fraud case."

Connor relaxed. She was a public employee. There were never enough resources to do everything they or the public wanted the department to do.

"Now, how about lunch?" Kelly asked.

"Good idea. Any favorite places?"

"A lot of the lawyers go to that diner on Main Street."

"Then let's go somewhere else," Connor said.

THE SIDEWALK SLOPED downward toward the bay past many empty storefronts and one store that carried nothing but colored rocks they called crystals.

"How does that store stay in business?" Kelly asked.

Connor laughed. "I wondered the same thing when I first saw it." He held the door for her at a darkened Middle Eastern restaurant with booths separated by walls that didn't quite touch the ceiling. Eighties pop music played a little too loudly.

A young man sitting at the edge of a booth near the cash register handed them menus. "Sit wherever you want."

Connor walked toward a back corner and took the seat with his back against the wall and facing the front door. An older woman put napkin-wrapped utensils on the speckled table and stood silently.

"Falafel meal and coffee," Connor said never opening the menu.

"Same," Kelly said, "but with a pop."

The woman gave her a questioning look.

"Diet Coke if you have it."

The woman nodded and escaped behind a swinging door with a small window, then soon returned with a steaming mug and a large red plastic tumbler. She rushed away again without saying a thing.

"So, counselor. I'm pretty new here, a little over a year and a half," Connor said. "How about you?"

"Fifteen. Seattle before then. And you can call me Kelly. Except when we're in a big meeting."

"And you can call me Connor. Whenever you want. I was in Las Vegas. Way too hot for me."

"You grow up there?"

"Yeah. It's changed a lot. More people, more casinos, more trucks with billboards driving through streets crowded with more drunks. This is better. I envy people who grew up around here."

"Oh, I didn't grow up in Washington. Chicago. Mt. Rosewood neighborhood if you've ever heard of it."

"I have not. What's its claim to fame?"

"Cemeteries."

"Really?"

Kelly laughed. "Really. And one of the last working farms in Chicago, although now it's a magnet high school."

Connor put his elbows on the table and leaned forward. "Pretty progressive—early entrants into the local food movement?"

"Yes to local food, although there are lots of farms around Cook County. Just not in Chicago. Not really a progressive place." Kelly looked out the diner's window, clearly uncomfortable. "I went to a parochial school in the neighborhood, I had very protective parents, but when the Chicago School District tried to expand the magnet school all sorts of people in the neighborhood came out to protest. Said terrible, racist things about the student body, how they wore funny hats and their pants too low. Parents, even those whose kids went to private schools said they needed to protect their children from bad influences and gangs."

"Including your family?"

Kelly looked at the table as she nodded. "My dad."

"Huh. I always thought it was a cosmopolitan place. And diverse."

The young man dropped paper plates filled with falafel and rice on the table and disappeared.

"Chicago has lots of ethnic neighborhoods, but not much mixing. At least when I lived there twenty some years ago. Mine was an Irish neighborhood and there were Germans and Polish and Dutch and Italian neighborhoods. Nobody cared too much about them, but if a Black family moved in, there was trouble. Despicable stuff—cross-burnings, name-calling, eggs on any car they dared to park in the driveway. My parents moved just after I moved out here, so when I go back, I don't see the old neighborhood." Kelly shifted on the uncomfortable bench.

"Ever think about moving back?" Connor asked as he spooned a little tahini onto his falafel.

"Never."

"Me neither. Las Vegas is for rattlesnakes and scorpions."

"And the mob?"

Connor shrugged. "Organized crime is everywhere. What do you think about Galmenberg?"

"I'm happy here, settled. It's not as cold or snowy as Chicago. How about you?"

"A little gloomier than I anticipated, but I was done with the dry heat. Is your husband from here?"

"No husband, just me and my daughter Ruth," Kelly said with a finality that told Connor not to prod.

Kelly finished her food quickly. "I probably better get back." She took a twenty from her wallet and slid it toward the slip of paper the young man dropped on the table as he rushed past.

"That's too much!" Connor protested.

"You can pay next time," Kelly said.

"I'd like that," Connor said, smiling.

CONNOR WASN'T SURE what to make of Kelly Flynn. Direct but cautious, like most of the attorneys he'd ever met. He thought about his dad and friends on the uphill hike back to the sheriff's office. Prosecutors and defense attorneys might be playing for different teams, but all of them were wary, suspicious, friendly when they weren't in front of a jury, assertive when they were. *Do they teach that in law school, or was that just the personality type?* Whatever. It would be good to have a friend in the prosecuting attorney's office. He wondered how she looked when she wasn't in the bland uniform of most courtroom attorneys.

I'll call the Nininpak officer before filing this away, Connor decided when he saw the still open folder on his desk. He dialed his phone.

"I know Aunty Therese is worried," Sweka said when he picked up. "But she and Dee really didn't get along since Uncle Vern died, and they don't talk much since Dee moved out."

"Diyanni, Dee's your cousin?" Connor asked.

"Distant, but our moms are pretty close."

"Did you talk with Dee when you saw her at the Casino?"

"No, she waved when she first got there. That's when I saw her. I was doing security that night. Dee seemed fine, smiling and chatting with the other women she was with."

"Is Dee the kind of girl who would disappear for a couple of weeks?"

There was a long silence before Sweka responded. "She's pretty independent, and she and Tyler, that's her boyfriend, have a rocky relationship."

"Can you tell me more about Tyler and her friends?"

"Other than Memorial Day, I hadn't seen her in a long time. All I know is what my mom tells me, which isn't much. Dee's three years younger than me, so she was a freshman when I was a senior in high school. She was pretty and popular, had gone to elementary school in Seattle and so was cooler than the rest of us. I was somebody who faded into the background. She started hanging out with Tyler and his crowd toward the end of that year. I went to school in New Mexico for a couple of years after graduation, and when I got back Dee'd moved to Galmenberg. I'm not sure who her close friends were then or later. I can ask my mom. She worked at the high school and would know."

"Galmenberg High takes in pretty much everybody around here, right?"

"Yes. We had a long bus ride."

"Is Tyler Nininpak?"

"No. He's a white kid from Galmenberg."

"Thanks, Daniel. We'll keep the missing person's file open here, and let me know if you need my help."

"I should tell you it's not my case. I told Aunty Therese I'd seen Dee to make her feel better. I'm just a patrol officer. The BIA's Office of Justice Services would do any missing person's investigation."

"I'm waiting on a call back from them."

"Good luck with that," Sweka said. "I doubt they'll do anything until there's better proof something's happened to Dee that involves the Reservation."

"I can't interrogate any Indians without them, so I hope they do call."

"Anybody in particular you'd like to talk to? I could help with that."

"Could I look at those Casino security tapes?"

"That I can arrange," Sweka said.

FOUR

Thursday

KELLY FOLLOWED THE road along the bay as long as she could, her car window open to hear the waves crashing along the shoreline. She turned inland and saw glimpses of a snow-capped peak between the trees as she followed the Hotsaem River. The river was high and noisy as it ran over and past its rocky banks. She'd kayaked and rafted the river when she'd first moved here, thrilled by its wildness. The idea that she could try a rafting trip with Ruth flashed in Kelly's mind, and just as quickly vanished. She knew she wasn't in good enough shape anymore.

The landscape became rockier, the forest denser until suddenly the trees cleared into a vast parking lot. The Casino looked forlorn this early in the morning, its neon turned off and its parking lots containing few cars. Kelly turned onto a narrow gravel road just past the parking lot and drove for a few minutes until it dead ended near the river. Therese's house was a rectangular single level home with cedar siding weathered to an uneven gray. In front was a huge awning of slatted wood covered with a faded red canvas.

Kelly was surprised to see a Nininpak Tribal Government van parked in front. Therese opened the door before Kelly reached it. She was relieved to see Therese was dressed conservatively in black slacks, a gray sweater over a collared red shirt, and a long, single strand of red and black beads. Kelly admired Therese's silver cuff bracelet etched with a stylized coyote.

"My mother-in-law made it for me," Therese said, fingering its intricate details. She turned to let Kelly inside. "I wanted you to meet some people before we talked to Tyler and the Galmenberg police. They brought food to share. I hope you're hungry?"

Kelly realized she was and smiled. "Sounds good."

She followed Therese into an open room, one side lined with a chipped enamel sink, a small refrigerator and range, and in the center a cast iron wood burning stove.

"May I help?" Kelly asked.

Therese shook her head. "Sit. You're my guest."

Kelly walked to a fireplace along the opposite wall where several pictures of a young girl at different ages stood, one a smiling girl missing her front teeth, another the girl with long dark braids tied with red ribbons, a forced smile, and the same orca necklace as in the third picture, the portrait Kelly had seen on Tuesday. In between each was an unlit candle.

"Diyanni's necklace in these pictures is beautiful," Kelly said.

"Vern's mom was an artist," Therese said. "She made it for Dee when she started junior high school."

Three women sat in the open area between the stove and the fireplace.

An older woman with thinning white hair sat in a recliner covered with a bright colored blanket, a large orange cat on her lap. "Celia's pieces are in a museum in Seattle," she said, holding up her arm to display a cedar bracelet carved with several animals in faded red and blue and green. "She gave me this when Vern married Therese."

"Mother, this is Kelly, the lawyer I met," Therese said, and the woman's creased face softened.

"Nice to meet you," Kelly said, unsure if she should put out her hand. None was offered, so she decided against it.

The other two women sat on matching brown corduroy chairs, each with a covered plate on their laps. One in a navy blazer and pants stood as Kelly neared, and Therese took the plate from her hands.

"This is my cousin Layla," Therese said. "She's a manager at the Casino. And she brought us muffins."

"Our cafeteria bakes them every morning," Layla said, putting her hand out to Kelly. "I can take no credit."

"And this is another cousin, Tannis," Therese said, turning to the third woman. "You met her son, Daniel, on the beach on Monday."

"Yes, I remember," Kelly said. "Nice to meet you all."

Kelly folded a knitted throw over the back of a futon couch next to Diyanni's grandmother and sat there. The cat promptly joined her and pulled at the throw until it fell around her.

Therese gave everyone a muffin and a plate. She uncovered Tannis's plate filled with salmon jerky and cheese and put it on the center table next to another that held large slabs of bread and five unmatched mugs. The cat meowed loudly, and Therese shooed her out the door. Kelly hesitated over the jerky but didn't want to offend. It was surprisingly good, more tender than she'd expected. A little sweet, a little salty. She looked expectantly first at Therese, then at the other women.

"Daniel said a sheriff's detective is coming to the Casino tomorrow to look at our security tapes," Layla said.

"Detective Andino?" Kelly was surprised and pleased he was acting quickly.

"I think that's his name," Layla said. "You're welcome to join us."

"Thank you." Kelly looked at Therese.

"It would be good for you to come," Therese said. "I want to see them too."

"Daniel invited him," Tannis said, pride evident in her voice. "He's at the Casino now going through the tapes again."

"We could ask Galmenberg Police to see them when we're there today?" Kelly said.

Therese scowled. "They won't come."

"Dee would not run away," Grandmother said in a soft but strong voice.

Kelly wondered if this were true. How could she ask without offending? She took a breath and folded her hands together. "She did leave to move to Galmenberg, didn't she?"

Grandmother's eyes turned angry. "Where was she to work? Who was she to marry? Many need to leave. That isn't running away."

Kelly nodded. Let the police press harder. She was here to be supportive.

They ate silently for a few minutes until Therese stood and picked up dishes from the small table. "We should get going. Tyler's probably still sleeping, so maybe we'll catch him before he leaves."

"You go," Layla said. "I'll straighten up."

THERESE DIRECTED KELLY to a small street filled with potholes and lined on each side with older cars and pickups, some with flat tires and many with cracked windshields and dented bumpers. No one walked the sidewalks, and curtains blocked every window. Therese pointed to a two-story, dirty-white wood frame house. Like most of the houses on the street, this one had two mailboxes nailed on the siding by the front door. After they rang the doorbell several times, Kelly heard the muffled clump clump of someone coming down carpeted stairs. A skinny young man in boxers and a rumpled T-shirt half-covering a sleeve tat of snakes and celtic knots answered.

"Tyler," Therese said.

"Hey," he said, opening the door wider. "Dee's not here."

"Can we talk?" Therese asked.

Tyler led them upstairs to a stuffy apartment, gathered papers and an empty pizza box off the couch, and motioned for them to sit. All the chairs faced a huge flat screen TV, the only thing in the apartment that looked new. Tyler sat in a recliner and lifted its footrest.

"I came by last week to see Dee, but nobody answered the door," Therese said.

Tyler shrugged and leaned his head back as if talking was too much work. "She hasn't been around in a while."

Kelly watched a large roach climb the faded yellow striped wallpaper behind his head. She had to control her wish to bolt.

"When did you last see her?" Therese asked.

"You a cop?" Tyler said to Kelly.

"No."

"Last time was Memorial Day. She was going to a party at the Casino with her work friends. I wasn't invited."

"Didn't you worry when she didn't come home?" Kelly asked, pushing up her glasses.

"She stays away sometimes," Tyler said. "She's a free agent."

His girlfriend's missing, and this is all he has to say? Kelly needed to be sympathetic. Warm. Wasn't sure she could.

"I don't think she did a runner," Tyler said. "Her stuff's still here."

"Everything?" Therese asked.

Tyler nodded.

Wasn't that a clue she planned to come back, you moron? Kelly wanted to say.

"Tyler, was Diyanni a sex worker?" Kelly could feel Therese stiffen and shift on the couch.

"Are you asking if my girl was a whore?" Tyler showed energy for the first time.

The police will certainly ask. "You said she was going with her coworkers. Where did she work?"

"She does nails over at that spa on 59th."

"Did she do drugs?" Kelly asked.

"Weed sometimes," he said. "Maybe something else at a party."

Kelly sensed he wasn't telling the whole story, knew he probably wouldn't.

"I want to talk to her friends at the spa," Therese said. "Do you know their names?"

"She mentioned a Pinny a few times."

"Can we take a few of her things?" Kelly asked.

"No problem. It's all in there." Tyler motioned toward the next room.

"Why are we doing this?" Therese whispered as she looked through Diyanni's closet.

"The police will want DNA," Kelly said as she used a tissue to pick up a red comb and a pink toothbrush she hoped was Diyanni's then put them into one of the plastic bags she'd brought. She rummaged through a pile of clothes on the floor and found several lacy panties and took those too.

"Dee had a necklace her grandmother gave her," Therese said to Tyler as they were leaving. "I couldn't find it."

"She wore that all the time. I'm pretty sure she had it on when she left," Tyler said.

When they got into her car, Therese slammed the door, crossed her arms, and stared out the windshield.

"You're upset," Kelly said.

"Dee's a good kid," Therese said turning to Kelly, her mouth clenched. "Impetuous, naïve. But not a prostitute. Is that what you think? An Indian living in the city must be a prostitute?"

"No. I'm sorry. I thought I should ask."

"It's insulting. Officer Fisher probably thinks the same thing and so won't do anything."

Stunned, Kelly considered the truth of that. Kelly had heard rumors the spa was much more full-service than nails. Police raided it on more than one occasion. She assumed they did at least some legitimate business, probably to launder money her most cynical self was sure. She decided not to mention any of this. The police would know. Therese didn't need to. And Kelly felt a sting of embarrassment at her glib assumptions.

"You're right. Why don't you ask the questions when we talk to the folks at the nail spa?" Kelly said. "I'll try to just listen."

THE NAIL SPA was in an old neighborhood of run-down storefronts with apartments above. They parked in front of a row of multicolored stores. The spa was painted forest green and had a neon sign flashing "Open" on the door. On the front window were the words "Walk-in Massages Available" and a silhouette of a shapely woman that reminded Kelly of truck mudflaps she'd followed on the interstate.

The sharp smell of acetone accosted Kelly as the front door jingled their entry, and a small woman in a white lab coat rushed toward them. The shop was practically empty. The only others were a tall dark woman in a loose pink short sleeved smock and wearing rubber gloves in front of an older white-haired woman sitting in a large, padded chair.

"Is Diyanni Hupt here?" Therese asked.

The woman looked confused. Therese pulled out her picture.

"Ah, Dee. No."

"I'm her mom," Therese persisted. "I can't find her. Have you or anyone here seen her?"

"No. We fired her."

"Fired her? Why?"

"She didn't come to work."

"When did she first miss work?" Kelly interrupted.

The woman ran to the rear of the shop and disappeared into a back room.

"Can we talk with Pinny?" Kelly called after her.

The tall woman lowered the sitting woman's feet into a tub of bubbling water. She pulled her long black ponytail behind her back as she ambled toward them. "I'm Pinny. I could fit you in in an hour."

"We just need to know if you've seen Dee."

"I'm on break in an hour," Pinny said and pointed to the diner across the street.

Kelly tried her best to hide her distaste when they entered the diner. Nothing about it appealed to her, not its torn red vinyl benches or scuffed gray tables. Not the dirt accumulating at the baseboards or the heavy smell of bacon and fried food. Not the greasy haired cook leering at them through the opening between the counter and the kitchen. She ordered a cup of coffee and a bowl of chili, figuring those were safe. She reminded herself that Guy Fieri liked neighborhood holes-in-the-wall. It didn't help.

As they waited, Kelly found talking with Therese difficult. Therese didn't volunteer information, said little, didn't ask questions. Therese hardly ever looked at Kelly, and her face didn't change from its calm mask. "Did anything happen with you and Diyanni?"

Therese looked at Kelly for a second before focusing on the space next to her.

"I've got a teenage daughter," Kelly said. "I know she wants to leave the second she can. I always wonder what I've done."

Therese relaxed and gave a weary smile. "Teenagers."

"Some teenagers like their parents. I keep wondering if I'm missing something or doing something wrong."

"Everybody hides their trouble."

Stymied, Kelly tried again. "It probably doesn't help that Ruth's adopted. And an only child. Does Diyanni have brothers and sisters?"

"No," Therese said, a bit of sadness littering her voice.

"I'm just trying to understand why she moved, why Tyler thinks she might have left town." Kelly reached for Therese's hand, but missed it as Therese dropped her hands below the tabletop. "Was her dad around when she left? Is he why she left?"

Therese glared at Kelly as she picked at the french fries the surly waitress put in front of her. "Vern died when she was fifteen. They were great together. She left because she wanted reliable hot running water and good wifi and Tyler."

Kelly blushed as she crumbled saltines into the watery tomatoes. "I'm sorry. That must have been hard."

"Dee was mad when we moved back to the rez when she was twelve. Said we ruined her life," Therese said.

Kelly sat silently, hoping for more. When no more came, she asked, "Why'd you move back?"

"They're our people," Therese said, looking as if she'd never heard such a stupid question.

"Why'd you leave?"

"Vern lost his job when the first Casino closed. He tried fishing and clam digging with his brothers but too many others did that and none of them could make any money. The only job he could find was at a factory near Seattle. Nobody hired me. Then the factory laid him off. Vern felt he'd failed. It was a hard time. When the new Casino opened, we moved back. We had to go. We wanted to. Dee was too young to understand."

Guesses and sympathy swirled in Kelly's head. She knew her mom had made many choices for her dad that Kelly felt had hurt her. She had more sympathy for her mom now than back then.

The waitress was all smiles when Pinny joined them. Cheeseburger and french fries. A chocolate malt. Cherry pie.

"Best pie in town," Pinny said, turning to Therese. "So, you're Dee's mom?"

Therese nodded.

"And who are you?" Pinny said to Kelly. Pinny took off her jacket and revealed a tattoo of a large feather with small birds emanating from its tip. "You don't look related. If you're police, you can leave now."

"I'm a friend, helping her look," Kelly said. "Tyler told us you might have gone with her to a party the last time he saw her, on Memorial Day."

Pinny's food arrived, and she ate with a speed and gusto Kelly hadn't seen since Ruthy was six.

"Yeah, that was the last time I saw her too," Pinny said between bites. "It was a work thing at the Casino. Pretty girls serving drinks to high rollers and businessmen. It was crowded and busy. She told me a guy offered her a waitressing gig at an after-party. I told Dee don't be stupid, but I could tell the extra money tempted her. Guess she needed it for something."

"She asked me for money to take classes," Therese said.

Pinny looked at Therese with pity in her eyes. "She seemed more desperate than that."

"Did you know the man?" Kelly asked.

"No. I didn't get a good look at him, just saw he had gray hair." Pinny picked up a piece of burger that had fallen on her plate and licked her fingers. "I think she said his name was Jerry. Or Harry. Something like that. I don't know if Dee went with the guy. All I know is she didn't ride back with the rest of us."

When Pinny finished her meal, she waved at the waitress and asked for her pie to go.

"Gotta run. Thanks for lunch," she said as she got up to leave. "I hope you find her."

THE GALMENBERG POLICE Department filled a city block not far from the sheriff's office. The sirens and street noise dimmed as Kelly and Therese entered, and the heavy doors enclosed them in a sterile lobby, the only human visible sitting behind heavy bullet-proof glass. Therese's agitation grew as ten, fifteen, thirty minutes passed. Kelly was sure Officer Fisher was making them wait to intimidate them.

"I'm glad we talked with Pinny," Kelly said. "That party seems important. It'll be good to see those security tapes."

Therese nodded.

Finally, one of the many doors opened. A stocky man with a buzz cut, wearing a short sleeve navy shirt with insignia on each arm and a silver badge near his collar waved them in. A huge gun pulled his belt down along one side.

"Nice to see you again, Therese," he said, clasping her hand into his two huge ones.

When it was clear he wasn't going to acknowledge Kelly, she thrust her hand toward him. "Officer Fisher? I'm Kelly Flynn. We spoke on the phone."

Fisher looked at her, then led them past desks filled with people talking on phones or staring at computers to a small room surrounded by glass on three sides. It was bare except for a metal table and four chairs, a pad of paper and a pen. He held the chair for Therese, then sat in one across the table.

Kelly put her briefcase on the table with a satisfying clunk and pulled out her file before she sat. It gave her time to quell her irritation. No sense starting that way.

"Officer Fisher," she said in her most pleasant negotiating voice. "We just want to help."

Fisher stiffened, then he, too, seemed to think better of it. He spread his hands on the table as if to show he wasn't hiding anything. "I'm sure that's true."

"It's been two weeks since Ms. Hupt reported her daughter missing, almost three since her boyfriend and work friend last saw her. We're hoping you have ideas about what to do next. We want to help, organize a volunteer search, work with your public information officer. Get her picture out there, on the news."

Fisher stretched his huge body and put his hands behind his head, elbows like wings protruding from his neck. "Where do you suggest we start?"

Kelly found his approach bullying and condescending, but he wasn't wrong. Where would they start? "Have you shown her picture throughout her neighborhood already? Looked at security videos in the stores she frequented? Requested the Casino security tapes since that's the last place she was seen?"

Fisher dropped his arms to the table and leaned toward Therese. "Listen. I'm sorry your daughter hasn't called you. But she's an adult. She's not disabled. We have no reason to think a crime's been committed, and if there's no crime, we can't help you."

Shock waves ran through Kelly's body. "Who is the detective assigned to the case?"

"There isn't one."

"We'd like to speak to the detective in charge of your special victims unit," Kelly said, clenching her hands.

"I'll see if he's here." Fisher sauntered out of the room.

Kelly paced, her mind filled with anger and disbelief and plans of what she could say to the detective once he deigned to arrive. Again, they waited.

"They haven't done anything," Therese said, more a statement than a question.

Kelly shook her head.

A large man with piercing eyes and a white stubble beard came in carrying a laptop and a thin manila folder, followed by a young woman in blue carrying a pitcher of water and several paper cups. He smiled first at Therese and then at Kelly. Her righteous anger deflated when he shook their hands then asked them to sit.

"I'm Detective Olafson. Officer Fisher tells me your daughter has been missing since Memorial Day?"

Therese nodded.

When everyone was seated, the detective handed Therese a brightly colored brochure, *Your Loved One is Missing!!!*

"I know you're worried and frustrated," Olafson said, "but until we have evidence of a crime, there's not much we can do. There are lots of reasons she might not have gone back to her boyfriend. Is there anything else? Missed appointments?"

"She missed work and was fired," Therese said.

Olafson nodded. "That's concerning. Did she pack her things?"

"It seemed like everything was still in her apartment."

A worried crease formed between Olafson's eyebrows, and he asked several more questions: was she depressed? *Yes.* Had she run away before? *Yes.* Was she having financial problems? *Yes*. By the end of the questions Kelly was convinced Olafson was concerned.

"I'm glad you came back in," Olafson said. "After thirty days state patrol asks us to get more information and we'll file a report with them. Would you be willing to give us a DNA sample?"

Therese nodded, and the assistant handed him a swab and a glass tube.

"We'll need a sample of Diyanni's DNA if you can get one."

Kelly handed him the hairbrush, toothbrush, and panties. "We got these from her apartment."

"Great," Olafson said. "Any other close relatives who would give us DNA?" Therese nodded. "Tell them to come in, or we can meet them somewhere. Can you get us her dental records?" He handed Therese a consent form.

These questions chilled Kelly. This information would help identify a body. It wouldn't do anything to help find Diyanni alive.

Olafson verified the information Therese gave in the original report and asked gentle questions about Diyanni's lifestyle. When he tried to add Diyanni to the National Missing Persons' database, he found she was already there.

"Tribal police must have entered Diyanni into this database," Olafson said. "I'll supplement it with what we've talked about today. Let's register both of you so you can search it too."

"I met yesterday with the head of the county's missing persons' unit," Kelly said. "He might have done it. And he told me he's interested in a task force for this and other cases."

"I heard the county had a new guy. What's his name?" Olafson asked.

"Connor Andino."

"I'll give him a call."

Therese showed Olafson the posters she'd tried to circulate, and Olafson agreed neighborhood patrol officers might have better luck getting local shops to post the picture. He promised a press release and to contact the sheriff's office and the state patrol.

Kelly wondered why this hadn't been done already but kept quiet.

Olafson suggested posting on social media, and when Therese said she didn't have regular access to the internet, Kelly reminded her Margarete had already done it.

"Is Ms. Flynn your legal representative?" Olafson asked.

Therese turned toward Kelly, a question in her eyes.

"Technically, no," Kelly said. "I work for the prosecuting attorney's office, but this isn't one of the office's cases. I'm helping Therese."

Olafson frowned and turned to Therese. "Do you want Ms. Flynn to interact with us on your behalf?"

Therese nodded. "I don't have a car or a computer and cell service doesn't always work at my house, so if she's willing . . ."

"I'm willing," Kelly said.

Olafson pulled an authorization form from one of his files and had Therese sign it, then asked Therese more questions. When Therese told him the last time anyone had seen her was at the Casino, he sat back in his chair.

"A missing Nininpak woman last seen on the Reservation," he said, frowning. "We may have a jurisdiction problem here. Have you reported her missing to the tribal police?"

Therese nodded. "When she was first missing. They told me to come here because she lived in Galmenberg. I filed a report with the sheriff too."

"Officer Daniel Sweka at the Nininpak Tribal Police Department knows about the case if you want to talk with someone there. I got the impression he'd be grateful for the help." Kelly took out a business card and wrote her cell phone number on the back. "And here's how you can get a hold of me.

Tomorrow we're going watch the Casino's security tapes from the party, see if we can find out who Diyanni left with. We hope you'll join us."

"I'll need to see," Olafson said. "If it doesn't work out, have them send me a report."

FIVE

FRIDAY

SLOT MACHINES CLANGED a noisy welcome when Detective Andino entered the Casino Friday morning. Women carrying half-filled plastic cups on trays wandered between the rows of slot machines making their circus sounds. Cigarette smoke choked him, and he realized it had been a long time since he was anywhere with people smoking with such abandon. Haze hovered over the flashing lights atop the machines while dead eyed men and women, most of them older, pushed buttons on the noisy machines in front of them. Several sat between two machines, and all were drinking from clear plastic cups while they watched pictures spin on the screen. Why a beautiful place like this wanted to imitate Las Vegas was beyond him. *Money,* he reminded himself, *it's always about money.*

Connor saw Kelly near the cashier's station and lifted his hand to her. A woman and a uniformed man Kelly introduced as Therese and Officer Sweka soon joined them. An elevator behind the cashier brought them into the offices on the Casino's second floor. A small woman in a gray suit rushed toward Therese and hugged her.

"We'll find her," the woman said, then pulled away and thrust her hand toward Detective Andino. "Layla Mos, Casino Manager. Welcome." Warmth and concern exuded from Layla's troubled eyes.

"Connor Andino. Thanks," he said.

Layla pointed to a laptop on the conference table and turned on a projector from a remote in her hand, suddenly business-like. "Daniel told me Dee was here for the Memorial Day party, and he's reviewed the tapes from that night. We have a lot of cameras on the gaming floor and one at every entrance, but only a couple in the private party rooms and on the rooftop patio."

The first clip showed five women and a small man entering a ballroom decorated in flags and stars and patriotic bunting. Along two walls were bar stations with young men in white shirts and flag bow ties, opening wine bottles and setting glass jars with dollar bills next to them.

Therese caught her breath and pointed to a young woman in a snug red dress turned toward the camera as she walked toward a table being loaded with cheese and shrimp on ice. "That's Dee."

Kelly pointed to a stunning woman in a blue dress with scattered sequins that mimicked the night sky. She whispered to Connor, "That's Pinny. Therese and I talked with her on Thursday."

"I hope you took notes," Connor said.

"I'll send you an email."

Connor noticed how pretty Diyanni was, her long dark hair shimmering with red highlights in the bright lights, and her confident stride. He wondered if the confidence was real or a show for the room.

"We invited the high rollers," Layla said. "Mr. Kam, that's the man with Dee, and a few local businessmen invited others." Layla focused her laser pointer on a short woman next to the man. "That's Mrs. Kam."

In the next clip the room was crowded.

Diyanni walked from group to group bringing flutes of something bubbly, laughing and touching the elbows of men who spoke to her, leaning closer toward those who put bills on her tray. Connor saw Therese stiffen. Kelly glimpsed an attorney she recognized and pointed him out to Connor who nodded and wrote down the name. Diyanni didn't stay long with any one group, and Connor watched her red dress weave through the crowd even when he couldn't see her face.

In the last clip, the crowd was rowdy. Diyanni stood near a bar stand, talking to a man with shaggy gray hair hanging just below his ears facing away from the camera. Connor hoped they'd let him look through the whole tape for a face shot.

"We'll need names," Connor said. "And I'd like to see the full tapes for that day. The Casino floor too. Would it be possible to see the room where the party was?"

"Sure," Layla said and led them to a large room where workers in black and white uniforms were setting tables. "This is our largest private room. We rent it out for parties, banquets, dances, and any big gathering."

Connor scanned the room.

"There are cameras at each of the three main doors, the door to the prep area, and at the back exit," Sweka said, pointing to each. "When there's a crowd it's difficult to see faces, especially in the middle of the room."

Connor strode toward the far end of the room near a back exit. "This is where the buffet tables were?"

"One set, yes," Sweka said. "There also were tables in the middle."

Connor opened the exit door to a small landing above steel and cement stairs. The group followed Sweka into the prep room, which was little more than a large closet. Shelves with folded tablecloths, baskets of silverware, napkins, and condiments lined two walls. Elevator doors filled a third.

"Where does the elevator end up?" Connor asked.

"The kitchen," Sweka said.

"No cameras in here?"

"Not in here, no. There are in the elevators and in the kitchen. We didn't find any footage of Dee leaving, but you're welcome to try," Sweka said, handing Connor a flash drive. "I know your video capabilities are better than ours."

"Thank you," Connor said. "We can watch them together on our equipment."

"I'd like that," Sweka said.

"I saw you put Diyanni's information into the missing person's database," Connor said. "What other bases have you covered?"

"We've alerted the BIA and the FBI," Sweka said, "but so far they've shown little interest. We've set up a search tomorrow for the surrounding area."

"I'm finishing up an email on who we talked with and what we learned yesterday," Kelly said. "I'll give you my impressions, but for sure you'll want to talk to them too."

"Will you copy me on that email?" Sweka said.

"Of course," Kelly said.

"Let's hold a press conference this afternoon, get the public's and the media's attention, as soon as we can," Connor said. "We've already lost a lot of time. Maybe somebody saw something."

CONNOR AND OFFICER Sweka decided to hold the press conference at the Cascadia County Criminal Justice Center in Galmenberg, figuring more news outlets would show up there on short notice than on the Reservation. Exactly at two, Connor filed into the press briefing room with Therese, Sweka, Sheriff Nisser, and Galmenberg police. One long white plastic table with several folding chairs filled the space next to a fixed podium raised two feet above the rest of the room. Therese kept a stoic face, her body stiff, her hands clasped tightly underneath the table.

Kelly and Layla sat in the front row of folding chairs on the white laminate floor and smiled encouragingly at Therese. Several reporters approached

Kelly as the group on the dais organized themselves. Connor heard her say "no comment" several times. One reporter tried to talk with Layla, but she refused to look at him. The reporter took the seat next to Kelly as Sheriff Nisser tapped one of several microphones on the table.

The Galmenberg Police Chief, a thin man in full dress uniform, medals gleaming, walked to the podium, put his hat on the table next to him, and ran his fingers through his thick gray hair. His stance exuded authority. Just before the press conference, Connor had read Kelly's email telling him Galmenberg Police had shown little interest in this case. Until the cameras were on, apparently. The chief's face was suddenly brighter when a bank of lights in the rear of the room came on.

"Hello, everyone," the chief began in a booming voice that reminded Connor of a radio announcer. "We're here to ask your help finding a missing Nininpak woman who has been living here in Galmenberg the last few years, Diyanni Hupt."

Diyanni's high school graduation picture shone on a screen on the chief's side as he talked. "She's twenty-two now." The picture shifted to a more recent snapshot of Diyanni grinning as she stood with a volleyball in her hand, her hair tied into a long ponytail. "We're working alongside the sheriff's office and Nininpak Police, so I'll let Officer Sweka take over from here."

Sweka gripped the podium and shifted his eyes too quickly around the room as he talked. "Diyanni Hupt lived on the Nininpak Reservation with her mother, Therese," he gestured to Therese, "until she moved to Galmenberg three years ago. She was last seen at a party at the Casino on Memorial Day." The security tape picture of Diyanni entering the Casino with Mr. and Mrs. Kam, Pinny, and two other women flashed onto the screen. "If you saw her that night or after, or if you have any information about where she might be, please call me or any public safety department." Phone numbers for the sheriff's department and the Galmenberg and Nininpak Police Departments shone on the screen. "We've started a search around the Casino and want to expand it. If you'd like to help, please call one of the agencies on the screen so we can coordinate." He turned and asked softly, "Therese, would you like to say anything?"

Connor pulled a microphone in front of Therese, and its screech filled the room.

Therese stared straight into the television cameras. "Dee, please call me or Tyler or anyone to say you're all right," she said in a wavering voice as she pulled on the ends of her hair. "We're so worried." She didn't cry but couldn't say another word.

"Does anyone have questions?" Sweka asked.

The reporter next to Kelly asked, "Why do you think she's missing and didn't just decide to leave town?"

"She wouldn't do that," Therese yelled.

"She doesn't appear to have taken any of her belongings or money with her," Connor said, giving the reporter a withering look.

The reporters' questions were mostly unanswerable and seemed designed to provoke a reaction in Therese. After a few more, Connor stood, handed out a press release, and promised to keep everyone informed. Everyone at the table then filed out a side door.

"Are you OK?" Connor asked Therese once they were in the anteroom.

Therese nodded. Sweka moved next to her. "I'll get Layla and we'll head back."

SIX

The Weekend

KELLY HAD NO desire to go back to the office after the news conference. She remembered today was an early release day for Ruth, so texted to say she'd pick her up in front of the high school.

"Now?" was her reply.

"If you're ready."

"OK."

"Want to go somewhere?"

"No."

Just as well. The first news comes on at four-thirty.

"You get fired?" Ruth asked when she got in the car.

"Therese, the missing girl's mom, asked me to come to her news conference this afternoon."

Ruth looked at Kelly with interest. "How'd it go?"

"Fine. I'm hoping to catch it on Channel 2 tonight. Want to watch with me?"

"Sure." Ruth directed her attention to her phone, typed something into it.

"Popcorn, brownies, pizza?"

"We have brownies?"

"I have a box. I'll make them while you start on your summer reading assignments." Kelly pulled the car into the garage, centering it as best she could into the narrow gap between old bikes, broken furniture, and piles of boxes.

"Okay," Ruth said with a grimace. When they entered the house, Ruth climbed the stairs and shut the door to her room.

As Kelly waited for the news to start, she emptied the dishwasher. It was Ruth's job, but Kelly didn't want to risk the pleasant mood in the house right now. She wondered why she didn't take time off more often. Habit, she guessed. Work late, pick up something from a drive-through, hurry through dinner. She resolved to use more of the hundreds of hours of accrued leave she'd banked.

"What do you want on your pizza?" Kelly shouted up the stairs.

Ruth emerged and helped Kelly cut vegetables. "Skip the onions and meat on my half."

They sat on either ends of the couch to watch the news. The announcer was breathless about an accident this morning, a fire in California, a lost dog, a coming storm. At the commercial break, the announcer teased about the stories to come, including a quick picture of Diyanni.

"That's her," Kelly said. "Therese's daughter."

"Pretty," Ruth said.

Kelly cut the pizza during the weather report and yet another commercial. Babs meowed loudly until Kelly gave her a piece of meat from her slice. They had almost finished eating by the time the announcer read Connor's news release, asked for search volunteers, then went to a reporter standing in front of City Hall who played the clip of Therese begging for help in finding Diyanni.

"Studies have shown that Indigenous women go missing and experience a higher rate of violence and murder relative to their numbers in the population both in Washington and Canada," the reporter said. "A Canadian highway has been dubbed 'The Highway of Tears' because of the number of victims last seen or found murdered traveling on it. Many of the forty-nine Vancouver women Robert Pickton admitted to murdering were Indigenous."

"Why are Indigenous women so often victims?" the anchor asked.

"That isn't clear, but officials tell me they hope to find out," the reporter said.

"Because they've already disappeared to you!" Kelly yelled at the screen. "Racism. Poverty. Years of looking the other way."

"Calm down, Mom. The world will survive without your outrage."

If you're not outraged, you're not paying attention.

"This is why I don't watch the news," Kelly said. "They're always so facile. Let's give two minutes to someone's tragedy. Oops. Time's up. Let's have a heartwarming story about a kid selling lemonade." She stormed into the kitchen, mumbling her many objections. She needed a brownie. A glass of wine.

"Bring me a brownie," Ruth said. "A big one."

Kelly calmed some and put a plate of brownies on the coffee table. Babs sniffed them, then jumped between Kelly and Ruth on the couch. "I'm going to help search tomorrow. Want to come?."

Ruth shrugged. "I guess."

KELLY THOUGHT ABOUT Connor as she showered that night. It had been years since she'd been on a date. When Ruth was small, she blamed the difficulty of finding babysitters, but that excuse hadn't applied for several years now. The thought of dating made her tired, and dating coworkers was always a bad idea. Was Connor a co-worker? She met him at a work, but who else did she meet? In Seattle she'd tried internet dating but figured out quickly that most of the men she'd meet were not really interested in a relationship. So many tense evenings with little to say, so many lies when they said they'd call. The few that did call stayed for that heady first few months then disappeared. And then there were the dating scammers. She considered herself too smart for those, but those poor women probably had thought so too. Who had time to figure it out?

The last time Kelly was in love was her junior year in high school, almost twenty-five years ago now. Her parents were strict, her siblings annoying, her classes boring, but life was good because she was in love with Brad Clery, the quarterback at Brother Finnian High School. He took her to the Harvest Dance in his red Dodge Viper where they danced to Whitney Houston singing "I Will Always Love You." She was the envy of every girl at Mother of Mercy High School, the popular girls all wondering how Kelly could have made such a catch.

Kelly's da and ma knew Brad was a good Catholic boy, so didn't object to their spending hours in their unfinished basement with its concrete walls, plaid castaway couch and ancient television, a place so uninviting her normally curious sisters left them alone. Most of the time. They made out with abandon to the flickering light of *Roseanne*, *Cheers*, *Murphy Brown*, *Northern Exposure*. They always kept their clothes on, never knowing when someone might decide to check up on them, but it was thrilling when he would unbutton her shirt to kiss her breasts or slip his fingers down her pants. She did not want to pull away, but always did. Sometimes he would unzip his pants, and she would rub him through his boxers, his sex hard and sometimes peeking through.

"Don't be a tease," he'd whisper.

"Not here," she'd whisper back.

On the weekends they'd go to an early show, then drive south to the forest where cars lined a small lake in the dark. Here was her first time, on a freezing dark Valentine's Day a few days after her sixteenth birthday, the anticipation and need turning to pain and fear and Brad's apologies and gratitude. If Kelly's da hadn't forbade her going out on a school night, she was sure Brad would have driven her there most nights, but as it was, they began skipping movies on Saturday night, going straight to the forest then heading to Venito's. Brad would have his arm around her when they'd walk in, a self-satisfied look on his face. Kelly wondered whether everyone could tell what they'd just done.

At confession she'd neglect to tell the priest her biggest sin, knowing she wouldn't stop, knowing she couldn't disappoint or lose Brad. The pleasure and guilt confused her. She hated when they sat with the guys from the football team, trying to be sociable with people she didn't know or didn't like while Brad ignored her except to once in a while put his hands too far up her skirt. Someone would always notice, and when she'd move Brad's hand further down her leg that someone would always laugh. But the strain of his muscles against her breasts when he held her made her body flare. She loved how afterward in the quiet of the car he'd kiss her and tell her he loved her as they'd make plans. Where he'd get a football scholarship, how she could visit on the weekends and then join him the next year. What kind of house they'd build in the country. He was her future, all she could think about.

Until that Sunday in late April when she realized she should have had her period by now. Fear made every nerve end buzz. No, it couldn't be. Brad was careful. When he forgot his rubbers, he'd pull out, or she'd give him head. No sense telling anyone until she was sure. But how could she buy a test? Everybody at the Jewel knew who she was. She didn't have a car. She couldn't ask Ma or Da or any of her friends.

After school Monday she took the bus to its last stop and started walking. When she was sure no one she knew was around, she went into the nearest drug store, bought a test, then went to their bathroom. She tried not to look at it while she waited but couldn't help but stare as a blue line slowly formed.

A current of panic jolted her. Made her unable to think or decide. Abortion was a sin. Legal. Available. But still a sin.

What would Brad say?

What would Ma say? Da? Her grandmas and granddas and aunts and uncles? Her little sisters?

Maybe abortion wasn't such a terrible sin. Maybe the sin was having sex before she was married, and this was the cure.

She thought about a billboard she'd seen. The wages of sin.

Kelly left the store in a daze, wandered up and down the street until the dull gray of the clouds began to darken. Commuters crowded the bus home, and the trip seemed an eternity but not long enough.

"Is that you, Kelly?" Ma said from the kitchen over the chaotic sounds of her sisters arguing whose turn it was to set the table. "Where have you been? Brad's been calling and I've been worried."

"Sorry, Ma. I decided to do my homework in the library," Kelly said.

Ma stood in the doorway, wiping her hands on a faded orange towel. Kelly's guilt rushed up her throat, and she ran to the washroom.

"Are you OK?"

"I'm not feeling well," Kelly said. "I think I'll lie down."

She begged off supper, told Brad not to come over when he called.

"Feel better, babe," he said. "See you tomorrow."

Tomorrow. Tomorrow she'd stay home from school. Use that spare test the company had so thoughtfully included. Maybe she'd done something wrong. Read it wrong. Tomorrow was another day.

Tomorrow it was the same.

Who should she tell first? Brad? Ma? Not Da for sure.

Brad, she decided. At least it wouldn't be entirely a surprise to him.

As they drove toward the forest preserve on Friday night, Kelly took a deep breath. "There's something I need to tell you."

Brad smiled. "What?"

"I'm pregnant."

Brad's smile withered, and he pulled into the first parking lot they passed. "Are you sure?"

"I took two tests but haven't gone to the doctor."

"Maybe you did them wrong."

"Maybe."

Brad dropped his head onto his headrest and closed his eyes, then banged his fist on the steering wheel. "We're too young to get married," he said, panic in his eyes when he finally looked at her.

"I know." Kelly reached for his hand, but Brad only grabbed the wheel tighter. She brushed a tear from her eye instead.

"I've got to play football in college to have any shot at the NFL," he said, looking out the window on his side.

"I know."

"Why weren't you on the Pill?"

Kelly looked at him, wide-eyed. It was her fault? "The priest says that's a sin."

Brad turned the car back on. "I'm taking you home. I've got to think."

They didn't speak on the ride home. Kelly clenched her hands and stared out the window, her insides churning. She really did feel sick. A half hour after she'd left, she was back home. Ma and Da were on the couch with a bowl of popcorn between them, her sisters and youngest brother at their feet.

"Still not feeling well, sweetheart?" Da asked.

"No," Kelly said, slowly climbing the stairs to her room.

Having a baby wouldn't be so bad. Aunt Christine was sixteen when Tara was born. She and Uncle Danny were doing fine. Kelly remembered holding Tara in her arms, amazed at the little hands and feet, loving dressing her up in frilly dresses or baby blue jeans.

Brad loved her. They could make it. It would be hard, but they could. They would.

Brad didn't call that night. Or the next. He wasn't at Mass on Sunday.

Monday morning, Kelly threw up, convincing Ma she needed to stay home another day.

Monday night Brad finally called.

"Can you come over?" Kelly said. "I miss you, and we have stuff to talk about."

"I think, well, I've got some money saved up."

Kelly's heart leaped. "I do too."

"I think us having a baby would ruin all our lives. Yours. Mine. The kid's. Nobody needs to know."

Kelly burrowed under her quilt and whispered, "You want me to kill the baby?"

"Don't think of it that way," Brad said. "Think of our future."

"I am," Kelly said, crying. "We can work it out. Lots of people do."

"I have dreams, Kelly," Brad said. "They won't happen if we get married now."

"They could," Kelly said. "They might take longer, but they could."

The silence between them stretched until Kelly felt it was choking her.

"I will pay. And go with you," Brad said.

Kelly cried, but said nothing.

"Will you make the appointment, or should I?" Brad asked.

Kelly hung up and buried her head underneath her pillow and quilt so no one would hear her cry.

Brad picked her up on a Saturday morning two weeks later, telling her parents they were driving to Madison to check out the University. Instead they drove to a clinic near the Wisconsin border where Brad thought it unlikely they'd see anyone they knew. They were mostly silent, Kelly staring out the window at the redbud trees' fragile beauty.

"Do you think it will hurt?" Kelly asked when they were almost there.

"I'm sure they'll give you something," Brad mumbled.

"No, I mean . . . the baby?"

Brad grimaced and said nothing. The muffler growled as he downshifted into the bleak neighborhood surrounding the clinic.

Kelly didn't remember much about the procedure, just flashes. Gray walls with a tint of green. Groups of women clustered around each other. Cold. Brad there but not there. And afterward, coming home late complaining she'd eaten something that didn't agree with her. Sleeping all day Sunday. On Monday she went to school to avoid her mother's concerned face, avoided her friends, came home, and slept.

Brad called for a while, late at night, his guilt bleeding from the phone. But he didn't come over. One Friday night she went to Venito's with a group of girls from school and saw him with Mary Sue, the head cheerleader at Mother of Mercy. Brad nodded and quickly looked away as if the sight of her burned his eyes. Mary Sue smiled a gloating grin.

"What happened?" her friends asked.

Kelly shrugged. "We decided it wasn't working."

Kelly was at Seattle U when she heard how Lorena Bobbitt cut off her husband's penis. She felt a surge of fury and a sudden bond. A welcome break from the lethargy she'd felt since the termination. Not that she could talk about it. No one knew except her and Brad. And God. She wondered on a scale of one to ten where her sin lay. Was Lorena's higher or lower?

For years, Kelly dreamed every night of a baby girl, bald, gaunt, blanched skin covered in blood, always crying. *Was that why my heart went out to Ruth crying in the social worker's office?* All she knew was she'd felt a fierce protectiveness for Ruth since that day that never went away.

SATURDAY MORNING WAS clear and cool as the crowd of volunteers gathered at dawn in the parking lot behind the Casino. Kelly and Ruth sat bundled in sweatshirts and hiking boots at a table with sign-in sheets for the volunteers. They gave each volunteer a reflective vest, a whistle, yellow tape, a bundle of orange flags on wires, adding nitrile gloves and a scavenging stick for those who hadn't brought their own. Therese stood near the edge of the parking lot with Layla and Officer Sweka and several other tribal members. Therese looked strong and determined and, as the crowd grew, hopeful.

"I want to look, not sit at a table," Ruth grumbled.

"We will," Kelly said. "Detective Andino said a patrol officer would take over when he got here, but they need to know who's here."

"Why?" Ruth asked.

"Because sometimes a kidnapper shows up to things like this," Sweka said, coming up behind them.

Ruth's eyes grew big. Kelly hadn't seen him arrive, but was glad for the explanation. "Which is why you need to stay with me, OK?" Kelly said.

Ruth nodded.

Deputy Springer arrived and offered to take their place at the table. Kelly could see Ruth's interest as she introduced them. *He's too old for you,* the voice in her head screamed and she was thankful the deputy barely said hello before introducing himself to two young blondes wearing UWA sweatshirts signing in.

"How do you decide who looks where and what group we should be in?" Kelly asked Sweka.

"We made grid maps last night to hand out to tribal members leading the groups," he said. "You can join any group you like. If you see someone you know, go ahead and join them."

"I've met you, Layla, Therese, Detective Andino, and Deputy Springer," Kelly said. "I don't see anyone else I know."

"Then join my group," Sweka said. "Therese's group is pretty big already with all her family members." He turned to Ruth. "How old are you?"

"Fourteen," Ruth said.

Sweka frowned. "It's probably not a good idea for you to search."

Ruth bristled. "Why not?"

"Because," Sweka paused, "you might find her."

"Isn't that the point?"

Kelly took Ruth's arm, hoping to prevent an escalation. "I'll take responsibility for her. I think I see teenagers in Therese's group."

"Yes." Sweka sighed. "There was no stopping them either."

Kelly wondered if she'd made a mistake inviting Ruth. What if they did find a body? Would it scar Ruth for life? She flashed on the gruesome pictures of bodies she'd seen as a prosecutor, the transcripts she read. She chastised herself for thinking this search would be a bonding experience and forgetting about how young Ruth was. She wanted Ruth to take the danger of being a young woman seriously, wanted her to be a good public citizen. It hadn't crossed her mind how awful it might be. *What a crap mother I am.*

By nine a.m. the crowd had divided into groups of around ten, each led by a police officer or a tribal member. Kelly suppressed a moment of glee when she saw Officer Fisher scowling with one of these groups. Sweka directed his group into a large white van with *Nininpak Tribal Government* painted in red on both sides.

"Mom," Ruth said before they got in. "Can you leave your fanny pack in the car? It's embarrassing."

"You're embarrassed now, but I bet you'll eat one of my granola bars or want some of my water pretty soon," Kelly said.

"Put them in your pockets," Ruth said, pulling out a small water bottle and a Snickers from hers.

"They're full too," Kelly said.

"Dork," Ruth said, but she smiled.

Four young men already seated in the van introduced themselves as being from the local college, and Kelly could sense Ruth was intrigued by their lanky, muscular bodies. A middle-aged couple joined them, both wearing ball caps with a Mariners logo. The young men soon started a heated discussion with the couple about what teams deserved to be in the World Series, a topic Kelly knew nothing about and had no interest in. As they drove a two-lane highway through the Reservation, she could see bits of water through the tall trees and an occasional cabin or trailer. She saw no farms and no people and wondered whether everyone had joined the search for Diyanni.

After a twenty-minute drive, Sweka pulled to the side of the road and asked everyone to stand in a line about arms' length apart.

"All you'll be doing is looking at the ground for anything that might show Diyanni was here. You've all seen the picture of what she was wearing the night she was last seen. It's all we've got to go on. If you see something, mark it with the yellow tape or one of your orange flags and yell or use your whistle for me so I can decide whether we should take a picture or collect something. Don't think of yourself as a CSI. We have too much ground to cover to worry about gum wrappers, beer cans, and other garbage. Concentrate on the big stuff: shoes, jewelry, pools of blood, body parts."

Kelly shivered. She was sure now Ruth shouldn't be here, wasn't sure if she should be. A grim quiet overtook them.

"We'll walk together at the same pace until we reach the water. Then we'll turn around and move to a new area to return from the water back to the road. We'll keep doing this for three hours, then head back." Sweka held up a map. "I'll keep track of where we've been so the next group knows what's already been searched. Any questions?"

Kelly raised her hand. "Are there any plants or animals we should watch out for? It looks pretty wild here."

Sweka smiled. "Good question. First of all, don't eat anything out here that you didn't bring. There are poisonous plants and berries and leaves, too many to try to teach you about right now."

Kelly laughed. "I promise."

Sweka looked at everyone. “All of you have dressed appropriately; I don’t see any bare skin other than faces, so you should be fine. My advice: check each other for ticks before we get back into the van. Watch out for thorns, of course. If you think you’ve touched poison oak or ivy be careful not to transfer the oils to your skin. Wear different gloves when you take off your clothes at home and wash them immediately and take a shower with lots of soap if you think you’ve gone through a patch. If you need to touch something on the ground, like when you put down tape or a flag, use your gloves. Leave them on all the time. And, yes, there are wild animals out here. The big ones, like bears, coyotes, cougars, will usually stay away from a group like ours but if you see one, stand still and announce the sighting. I’ll take it from there. Feral dogs and cats might approach, but if you wave your stick, you’ll be fine. If you’re allergic to bees, I hope you have your EpiPen.”

They shook their heads.

“This isn’t the wilderness part of the Reservation, County Search and Rescue are going there with the dogs, so just stay aware and you’ll be fine.”

The line of them moved methodically through the brush and between the stands of fir and alder trees. Kelly breathed deeply the sharp smell of pine needles mixed with smoke and sea air. She prodded the branches on small trees sprouting from the ground and moved aside the berries and fern-like plants hiding the forest floor. She’d never looked at the ground so closely before and marveled at the bugs and little frogs and salamanders crawling underneath the leaves. Many trees had lines of small holes running up and around the trunk. In the quiet of their sticks and feet swishing in the underbrush she heard birdsong, a two-beat call, a soft cooing, the piercing shriek of gulls as they neared the water. The beach was more rocky than sandy, some of the rocks a honeycomb of small holes. She saw bits of plastic and other trash mixed among the sea glass and branches. When she reached the waterline she turned around and waited for more instructions.

“Be sure to look among the rocks along the shoreline,” Sweka said. “Just a few days ago someone found a shoe with bones inside along this coast.”

Ruth grimaced at Kelly.

“No one found anything significant on this pass,” Sweka continued. “That’s a good thing, a hopeful thing. Let’s take a break before we move down the shore and head back toward the highway.”

“Hey, Mom,” Ruth said as they found a fallen tree to sit on. “Can I have one of those granola bars now?”

Kelly reached into her fanny pack and handed one to Ruth with a satisfied smile.

THE SMELL OF blood drew Traveler to the hope of food. He sniffed along the chain link fence that surrounded the smell and noise of machinery. He knew to avoid the opening lined with trucks and smoking men. He searched for loose ground to dig his way in. Two dogs joined his scrabble and wriggled through the fresh tunnel after him. They bared their teeth at each other and growled, separated, and looked for their chance to snatch any bit that might drop as a man dumped a barrel from the back of his truck into a noisy machine. One of the other dogs slunk toward a puddle of wet where a swarm of flies hovered, sniffed, licked, then slurped quickly. The man stopped loading and threw a rock at the dog, just missing. The dog ran behind a metal bin and peered outward.

Traveler crouched, looking for his opportunity, as a man in blue coveralls came from inside the squat metal building and lit a cigarette.

"What's in your batch?" the man said, waving the match and dropping it. The smoke drifted toward the line of metal vats where Traveler hid.

"Morning Donnie. Pig mostly, some chicken," the driver said, dragging another barrel off the truck bed.

Traveler twitched his triangle ears at a horde of flies, ready to jump or run. The barrel landed hard, and several scraps fell to the ground. The driver kicked them toward the building.

"You still doing your own butchering these days?" Donnie asked.

"Can't afford not to."

Donnie wrote something on a piece of paper, handed it to the driver.

The truck moved forward and the grinding noise stopped, Traveler and the dogs ran to the sandy area next to the building, grabbing whatever scraps they could, licking puddles of watery blood. Donnie smoked as he watched them, then threw a few pieces from the container inside the building to each dog. Traveler grabbed his and ran behind a dumpster, guarding his breakfast from the rats who peered at him from underneath a pile of sheetrock. Another truck pulled up.

"You're just encouraging them," the man in the truck said as he jumped from the cab.

"Rez dogs gotta eat too."

"Or you could shoot 'em. Put them out of their misery."

"Most of this will become dog food anyway. I'm just skipping a couple steps."

Traveler sniffed the lingering scent of human on his chunk then swallowed it in a single gulp. He licked the drips of blood that darkened his dirty white muzzle before they disappeared into his matted yellow fur.

HENRY

1998

HENRY WOKE TO silence and the sun shining through the crack in his bedroom curtains. Something was wrong. Mommy usually woke him in the dark to the smell of coffee and bacon. Why not today? He put on the jeans and sweatshirt Mommy laid out for him last night. He remembered hearing Mommy and Daddy arguing last night, doors slamming, glass shattering, the truck backfiring. Nothing strange. Where were they?

In the kitchen, his fear grew. The pot from last night's stew crusted in the sink, and silverware and their plastic dishes littered the floor. Mommy always put the dishes away. Henry felt cold, saw a broken window. The back door stood open. He remembered Mommy telling him to call 911 if anything happened. He lifted the phone, then saw Daddy's truck racing toward him. Daddy got out.

Where was Mommy?

"Don't you have school today?" Daddy asked, shoving Henry aside as he went through the door.

"Mommy didn't wake me."

"It's about time you got yourself up, made your own breakfast. Your mother's gone."

"Where'd she go?"

"Get to school."

Henry looked at the clock. 7:42. "I missed the bus."

Daddy swore. Took a loaf of bread and a jar of peanut butter from the cupboard. Filled a dented metal glass with water. "Get in the truck. You can eat on the way."

"I have to pee."

"Make it fast."

Daddy lifted Henry onto the cracked vinyl bench in the cab and threw his backpack on the floor, flattening the bread underneath. Daddy drove fast, and the bumps and ruts in the road made it hard for Henry to drink, so he put the glass between his legs and used his finger to eat the peanut butter. Daddy stopped in front of the school. No one was outside. As Henry jumped onto the sidewalk he saw the water had sloshed onto his pants between his legs. Once Daddy drove off, Henry sat on a swing in the playground, eating his bread and hoping his pants dried quickly. Soon the principal took him inside, combed his hair, took a hair dryer to his pants, brought him to his classroom. The principal shook her head at the teacher when she started to ask him where he'd been. Everybody stared as he sat down and the kid behind him poked him with the eraser end of his pencil.

Mommy'll be home tonight, he told himself.

But she wasn't. Not the next day either. Or the next.

When Grandma Janie called on Saturday, Henry cried.

"Waterworks won't help," Daddy said.

For the next few weeks, whenever Henry asked Daddy, the only answer he got was, "She's gone, that's all. She's not coming back. Now shut up and do your chores."

Where did she go? Henry wanted to know. Why did she leave me? Grandma Janie said she'd come today. Maybe she knew.

Grandma Janie arrived in a swell of dust and noise in a new yellow car. Or was it a truck? It looked to Henry like a car in front, but a truck in back.

"That damn woman always has to have the latest thing," Daddy mumbled as they watched her pull in.

She strode to the front door and opened the screen without knocking, then stood looking at Henry and Daddy, her arms crossed over her broad chest. Her hairline was damp with little beads of sweat climbing down her face. "Sam, Henry's coming with me. No arguments now."

"No, he's not," Daddy said, pushing Henry behind him with one arm and waving his fist in her face with the other. "I need him to help with the farm."

"I'll not have this child staying with you on this god forsaken farm. He's six! Look at him! He's too small to help. And when was the last time you washed his clothes? Gave him a bath? Cut his hair?"

Henry's face warmed with embarrassment. He'd give himself a bath tonight, ask Daddy how to work the washing machine.

"Go ahead. Get a lawyer. No court will give him to you, and you ain't going to kidnap him. Over my dead body."

"That'd be fine with me," she said, leaning to glimpse Henry. "What does the boy want?" Her voice changed to the wheedling whine some adults use when they talk to children. "Henry, you want to come with me or stay here?"

Henry peered at her in surprise. He had a choice?

"Henry wants his mama back, and that ain't happening."

"Yes, he needs a woman. Not a stinky old pig farmer and disgrace to our family name. It's no surprise to me she left. I'd a done it long ago. And Henry's too young to be mucking out those pens. He should be around boys his own age and play baseball." She leaned toward Henry and her voice became high pitched again. "Doesn't playing ball sound fun, Henry?"

Henry felt Daddy's body stiffen, could feel his rage coming on. He knew Daddy would never let him leave. "I like the animals here."

"Right," Daddy said. "We're done here."

Grandma Janie and Daddy glared at each other for what to Henry felt like forever.

"Get off my property or I'll have the sheriff drag you off," Daddy said, his voice soft and low and full of menace. He leaned over and stretched his arm to lift the phone hanging on the wall.

"Oh, for heaven's sake, don't be so dramatic," Grandma Janie said, slamming the door as she left.

Henry fought the sting of tears forming.

"Don't cry. You're a big boy." Sam lifted Henry to his chest and put his chin on Henry's head. "Us men will get along fine without women slowing us down, right?"

2005

HENRY'S SHOULDER THROBBED from where his dad yanked him from his chair and thrown him onto to floor. He covered his head and crawled toward the door amid a flurry of kicks.

"Finish your chores!" Dad roared with a last shove out the door. "Those animals need feeding before you sit down."

"I gotta finish my project for school," Henry whined. Dad hated whining. Henry braced himself.

The blow came as a rake to his other arm. Warmth dripped underneath his torn shirt, and bile filled his throat.

"And how am I supposed to work when you've broken my arm and pulled out my shoulder?" Henry was scream-crying now.

"Figure it out, sissy." Dad stomped toward the barn.

In his mind, Henry planned revenge. He was almost as tall as Dad now. He could take martial arts. No, Dad would never pay for that. He could run away. Sleep in somebody's barn at night, move to a new one the next day. Someday he would.

The seven years since Mom left taught Henry to survive his dad's increasing anger and boozing and violence. He no longer blamed her for leaving. *But why didn't she take me?* he thought for the thousandth time.

Henry sat on the rough wooden porch and braced himself, knowing the pain to come. He bent his knee and gripped it with the fingers of his dislocated arm. Then he bent over his knee as far as he could and swung his shoulders back and forth until he heard the click that told him it worked. He threw up onto the dried mud next to the steps and breathed until he could stand. Then he turned on the hose, drank from it, and diluted the yellow scum until it soaked into the dirt.

Bastard. He went into the house and washed the other arm and wrapped his broken skin with an old T-shirt. *I should show this to the principal at school.*

But he wouldn't. When he tried to tell his fourth-grade teacher Dad hit him, police came to the school and a social worker talked to him, but nothing changed. Dad sweet-talked them, said, yes, sometimes he spanked little Henry when he disobeyed and no, he never hurt the boy. When it became clear to Henry he would be going home with Dad to an even greater punishment, he knew not to tell them about the broken arm last summer that Grandma Janie put a splint on. His arm still hurt sometimes, but no one cared when he winced during dodge ball. They thought he was a sissy too.

The pigs squealed as Henry dragged a large bucket of feed along the fence, then snorted as they rooted in the filled trough. He liked pigs. They were predictable. Friendly. Happy to see him. Not as beautiful as the cows, but to him the pigs seemed more intelligent when they looked at him as if they knew the ways of the world. Knew things he didn't.

Maybe Dad will die, and I can stay with the farm. The thought made him hopeful.

It was nearly dark when Henry returned the feed buckets to the barn, the lights from the kitchen just enough to illuminate the pump where he could wash off his boots before leaving them next to the stoop. The table was set, and his dad was pulling something out of the oven.

"I made tuna casserole," Dad said. "Your favorite."

2009

HENRY LEANED ON the fence surrounding the pig pen and thought about Gloria. Her wavy brown hair clipped out of her eyes with barrettes.

Her eyes the color of the sea before a storm. She smiled at him after class today. Should he ask her to Prom? He looked down at his dirty worn jeans, rubbing his cut and callused hands against his frayed jacket. No. A girl like her would never be seen with him.

Other girls would, he knew. A certain kind of girl liked the way his brown hair, streaked with gold from his days in the sun, was always a little too long, a little too messy. They watched the way his muscles flexed when he threw a ball, admired his perpetual tan when the rest of the boys were white from winter, appreciated the musk of farm that never left him. They even liked that he never smiled, never volunteered in class, never asked them out. They admired his worn blue jeans and faded shirts, thought him a rebel. A certain kind of girl liked bad boys, and the whole school decided he was one.

Except Gloria. She smiled at everyone, walked through the halls in a bubble of light. Kept her distance from the gossip and private jokes of the other girls, seemed not to notice when boys flirted with her. She was pretty in a comforting not a challenging way, soft curls around her face, not the severe slashes of straight hair the other girls found stylish. Like his mother, soft, timid, a bit frowzy. Only those eyes belied her calm, hinted at dark depths underneath. Henry was drawn to her, wanted to know if she too had secrets.

"Are those pens mucked out yet?" Dad yelled from the barn. "Do it now."

The worst job on the farm. Something Dad had done for many years. But Dad was wearing down, his hair stringy and graying, his walk slower, his back stooped. Still relentless and demanding, and that meant most farmworkers didn't stay. His dad had never been patient, and now he was a man who acted like life had cheated him, taken away the rewards due a hardworking man. He treated anyone who came and asked for work like slaves. No wonder they moved on as soon as they could.

Only Dad's buddy Cooley helped him out now and again. There was something menacing about Cooley, Henry thought, unsure why. His noisy, throbbing motorcycle? His oily grin? His bright, cheap clothes? His reptilian eyes? Neighbors told Henry that Cooley brought girls from Seattle and they had parties on those weekends Dad sent him to spend time with Grandma Janie. Henry wondered when Dad would decide he was old enough to party too. He'd be eighteen soon. That should be old enough. And he'd graduate high school in June. Maybe then.

Last week's rain left mud and puddles throughout the outdoor pens and invigorated the ever present stench of manure and rotting hay. The pigs rooted and snorted like kids at a water park. Henry put on his thigh-high boots and long vinyl gloves, dragged out a hose, and sprayed the worst of the dirt and straw off each pig, then swatted them into the barn. He raked back the straw from the wettest area of the pen and dug a trench to allow the puddles to drain outside the fence. His shovel hit something hard. He scraped around the blockage, releasing a sulfuric smell and felt the lump break. Not a rock, then. He wasn't going to let a few old tree branches stop him from making this job easier, so he dug around whatever it was as dirty water accumulated into the trench whenever he did.

He went back outside the pen to lower the outside trench and eventually only mud remained inside. He shoveled the manure from the corner the pigs favored into the large barrels they would carry to fertilize the fields. He lay a straw bale alongside the water trough but decided to clear out more of the sticks in his drainage channel before spreading the straw. A round, white object that looked more like a stone than a stick was barely visible in the muck. Henry dug around it with his hands, increasingly frightened when he held what appeared to be a part of a skull. Definitely not a pig's skull. If biology class had taught him anything, he was pretty sure it was human.

Henry dropped the skull and covered it with mud, then straw. When Dad called him in for supper, he said he wasn't feeling well and went to bed.

HENRY

2009

Boot camp suited Henry. He was used to someone yelling at him all the time for no apparent reason. He liked his shaved head, the rhythmic marching songs. Here no one laughed behind his back about his hair or clothes as everyone wore the same green camo, same boots, same underwear. All he owned and needed was in a footlocker next to his bed. Everything was orderly. He slept in clean, crisp sheets every night on a bed he made every morning. It calmed him to go to bed and wake up at the same time with his thirty bunkmates. Unlike them, rising at 0430 was easy for Henry who was used to morning chores. And everyone was too tired at the end of the day to talk much, which suited Henry fine. One guy from Texas talked enough for everyone. Henry just nodded at the silent wary ones like him.

Georgia was hot. Humid. Buggy. So unlike Northern Washington that still had frost the morning he left without a word to anyone. He'd signed up on his eighteenth birthday, took the tests, left for basic training as soon as he could.

After a week, the sweat and mud and mosquito repellent seemed his second skin. He smirked when other recruits wasted time in the shower covering themselves with the skimpy towel instead of letting the water slide off their pungent bodies. Henry had years of experience of having someone turn his water off too soon and made sure to quickly rinse the soap from his privates, armpits, head. No one ever mentioned the many scars along his back and legs.

Cleaning the head every evening after showers was new, and he reveled in the acrid smell of bleach after years of living with dirt and chaos. Every day was a physical challenge he met easily. He felt a little sorry, but mostly superior, to the city boys who thought their years of running and weightlifting provided sufficient preparation only to fall flat on their faces after crawling through mud and under fences or dodging between barricades. Henry ran and crawled and climbed, always focused. No time to think.

Henry's unit, less the three recruits who hadn't made it, started infantry school the day after basic training. Tex had lots to say about not getting any leave, but Henry had nowhere to go. When they learned of a local bar that never carded military guys, they celebrated graduation with an off-post trip. There, girls in summer dresses flirted with everyone in uniform. Henry felt dizzy from his first beer after ten weeks. He found it sad, the hilarity, the backslapping, the hopeful eyes of little tarts looking for the next Richard Gere—not that any of his unit were likely to be officers or gentlemen. After that first time, he and Cole and Trish stayed on base during liberty. Sometimes he thought about Gloria while masturbating, but he began to think he just had a weaker sex drive than most, particularly the guy they'd nicknamed Randy who loved to brag about his back seat conquests when the group returned wobbly and noisy after an evening in town. Henry decided his time was better spent doing push-ups and running, catching up on sleep, and memorizing manuals. He wanted jump school and knew he had to excel to have half a chance.

"Looks like the barracks rats got into airborne," Tex groused when the assignments list was posted. "You'd think they'd want real men."

HENRY BREATHED DEEPLY as the jump tower's pulley lifted him and the shouts and traffic noise diminished. Exhilaration. Joy. Sensations he could never recall having. The air seemed lighter, cleaner here than anywhere he'd been, and it made him lightheaded.

Fort Benning arched around him, its green, its tidy buildings, the busses in its parking lots, the other towers lifting his buddies on each side. For the first time in his life, Henry felt part of something good. Holy even. At the black hat's command, he released and dropped. His body jerked as the parachute blossomed in the mild wind.

Tuck head, feet together, bend knees, he repeated to himself. Face the wind. His ankle twinged as he rose and gathered the deflating silk.

"Again!" a black hat shouted. "Drop and do fifty."

Henry ran toward the tower. Joined the others in synchronized push-ups to the staccato of commands. *My people*.

His jump school buddies treated him with respect. Joked with him. Called him "Canuck" because the sixty guys in his bay decided he had an accent from living so close to Canada all his life. Now his unit had a private greeting of silently chopping their right hand in the air three times. Other units developed their own secret hand signals. Henry wondered what they meant. But all 650 of them acknowledged each other with smiles and hand grips.

Many had left after failing to pass the initial fitness tests. Many dropped out since, some unable to overcome their fear of heights, some injured after jumps from the towers. These defections made the rest of them feel strong, special, united. They repeated the exercises until jumping from a plane door, keeping their heads tucked and knees bent, landing on both feet then rolling became routine. A body response to the adrenaline dizziness.

His buddy Joe was on the lift next to Henry this time and gave Henry the hand chop. Henry copied the motion before releasing again. He landed first on his right foot and winced before shifting his weight to his left.

The thought of jumping out of a plane flying at 1200 feet and moving at 130 miles per hour next week alarmed Henry, but he pushed the fear out of his head. Rely on your equipment, rely on your training was his mantra. While most of his buddies celebrated in town, Henry ran and used the weight machines to strengthen his legs and ankles and arms. Sunday evening he taped his ankle, took one of the pills the medic had given him for pain, and went to bed early, barely hearing his bunkmates when they came in.

Jump days started early, long before first light. Everything the men did in the morning now seemed synchronized—sit up, feet on the floor, wash, shave, pee, get dressed, push everything into a locker, stay awake during the briefing, sing in cadence on the run to the harness shed, rigor shed, back to the harness shed. Help your buddy secure his equipment, submit to inspections, wait. Wait some more. Load onto a plane. Circle the field.

From his space along the wall of the crowded plane, Henry eyed the strained smiles of the others, knowing he too was trying hard to be brave. The noise and the earplugs made conversation impossible. The black hats called this first one a Hollywood Jump—a single jumper with a chute on his back and a reserve around his waist. At the signal, the first row stood up, hooked to the static line above their heads, and hurried toward the open door. At the green light, they handed their tether to the black hat standing there and jumped one at a time. At the red light, everyone stopped as the plane repositioned, then the march began again. Henry was in the third group. He followed the man in front of him. Just as he neared the door, the red light came on and the pilot circled back, giving Henry time to see the world spinning underneath. He forced himself to focus on the moment. Head tucked, knees bent and together. Stare at the horizon. When the green light came on, he gave up his tether and pushed himself out and away. The wind slapped his face, and he turned into it as one after another soldiers followed. The straps pulled on his shoulders and groin. Each second another's chute opened. Henry felt he was dancing in the air with his buddies, weightless and floating. Small white clouds dotted the sky, and the beauty of the world rushed in. Exhilaration. Joy. A perfect landing on both feet and a quick roll. He couldn't wait to go again.

The next day was a Combat Jump. Henry knew it would be more difficult with the added weight of a stuffed rucksack and weapons bag, but yesterday's jump gave him confidence. Today they loaded onto a smaller plane. Despite many fewer paratroopers, the plane was more crowded and uncomfortable than yesterday. Henry had little time to worry as he was the third in line to drop. Head tucked, knees bent and together. Green light. Jump away from the plane.

The propeller blast came as a surprise, disorienting Henry. Which way was the wind? As the harness strained, he watched the tree line and tried to turn. He struggled to climb his risers as the weight of his gear seemed to conspire with gravity to bring him closer to the trees and bogs surrounding the field as the ground rushed toward him. Using every bit of strength in his hands, arms, and shoulders he finally veered away from the tree line and dropped into a swampy part of the field, the uneven ground shifting his weight to his right foot. His buttocks forced a plume of water into the air and he rolled into a patch of squishy grass. He jumped up to tamp down the parachute and tried not to grimace as he ran toward the rally point.

"You all right, paratrooper," a black hat asked him.

Henry stood at attention trying not to favor his left foot. "Yes sir, Sergeant Airborne."

The sergeant nodded him toward the waiting bus.

"Hey, Canuck," Farm Boy, one of his buddies from Kansas, said, "you got mud on your face." Everyone on the bus laughed.

"Brown badge of courage," Henry said. "You don't think the field of battle will be clean, do you?"

"Ooh-rah!" one of the Marines shouted, and the high fives began.

Henry told his buddies he was going for a run, then joined several other paratroopers lined up at the infirmary. He knew he'd need more pain meds. The line was long, with those limping or unable to walk without support going first. He made sure he didn't limp or wince or grimace. His father had hurt him worse, and he survived that. The nurse iced his foot and insisted on an x-ray of his ankle, but the doctor said nothing was broken. Gave him an ace bandage, Oxycodone, asked him to stay off his feet for a few days. No way, Henry thought, they'll wash me out or send me back to start over. He told the doctor he'd be fine.

Wednesday morning was windy and drizzly, but still they rose before dawn and ran to where they put on practice rigs and jumped through mock airplane doors. The pre-jump lecture seemed particularly long to Henry as his ankle throbbed. He snuck another pill as he drank from his canteen. And then they waited. Six hours they waited, wearing their harnesses and holding their chutes, until they were ordered to the busses for the trip back to base. Henry hoped this day off his feet would make the final jumps easier.

EUPHORIA FILLED HENRY as his troop leader pinned wings to his uniform. He wanted to go to Afghanistan to expel those Taliban bastards from the face of the earth. Last night's combat jump had been difficult, but no one saw him shudder on landing, or that he rolled too quickly. He made it to the rally point, and that was what mattered. While his platoon spent time with family, Henry talked to the doc about pain in his knees and buttocks. The medic nodded knowingly and gave him a ten-day prescription, encouraging him to take one only when needed. Henry walked carefully out the door and took one with a swig from his canteen.

Henry hated to admit he had nowhere to go on his two-week leave before he needed to report to Ft. Campbell, so took a bus to West Palm Beach. He missed the ocean but had no interest in going someplace cold. At the station, everyone thanked him for his service, and an agent suggested several budget motels that gave discounts to military men, one that had a pool and wasn't too far from the beach. A taxi driver offered to take him there for ten bucks. Flush with the unspent pay in his bank account, Henry was determined to relax, swim, find some company. But first he intended to sleep. Stay off his feet. Watch TV.

The motel's pool was small, not much use for exercising but nice for cooling off. Henry didn't care about getting a tan but enjoyed stretching his legs on the lounge chair and feeling the sun on his body. Occasionally a mom with little kids played in the pool. Henry smiled as they did cannonballs and played Marco Polo, envied their unrestrained laughter. By noon it was too hot, so he showered then limped to a nearby Denny's. Across the street he saw a strip mall with a used bookstore next to a pain clinic and decided to buy a mystery to help him pass the time. The guy at the counter suggested *Black Echo*. Henry noticed the line outside the pain clinic kept growing, so he walked that way and looked in the door being held open by a thin man with a colorful sleeve tattoo on his left arm—waves, fish, a sailboat. *Very Florida*, Henry decided. *I should get a tat.* Inside were rows of plastic chairs, all filled. Young, old, well-dressed, unwashed. All waiting. *So much pain to treat*. He hoped he wouldn't need to join the line but was glad to know the place was nearby in case he ran out of pills before his pain subsided.

By the third day, Henry was restless and ready to explore. For four months he'd been busy and tired, with most of his time planned out for him. Now with the empty day in front of him his mind kept drifting back to his dad, the farm, the skull. No, he thought, enough. Keep busy. His ankle still made walking difficult, so he waited for the free trolley service. Henry talked with the driver of the mostly empty bus about becoming a paratrooper and the driver pointed out things Henry should do while he was in town. Henry got off at a park along the waterfront wanting to see the manatees. It was a long walk from the bus stop to the intercoastal waterway, but he was in no hurry. He stopped often on the benches strewn throughout the park and watched joggers and women pushing strollers. He got a hot dog and a root beer from a food truck and took another pill. It calmed him, made it easier to walk, made the colors brighter.

The same driver picked him up in the late afternoon. When Henry lamented not seeing any manatees, the driver said it might be too early. Not cold enough. He dropped Henry off at a local bar near his motel, saying it was where the locals went for great, inexpensive food. The bar was dark and nearly empty when Henry ordered a beer, wondering briefly if he'd be rejected, but the bartender didn't ask. The bar filled quickly. First came the older men and women sitting at tables and ordering meatloaf or pork chops, then men in baggy jeans and plaid shirts who took over the pool tables in the back, then younger men in khakis and short sleeves sometimes with women in floaty dresses.

Henry stood near the pool tables until someone asked him to play. After he ran half the table, the group bought him another beer, and they shared fries with burgers. Henry's anxiety evaporated, and he laughed more than he could remember. Several men left early, but the rest wanted to hear about the army. An old guy overheard and regaled them with stories of Viet Nam, but they mostly ignored him talking instead about the sad state of the country and where they'd been when the planes crashed into the towers. At some point a group of women speaking a mixture of English and what Henry guessed was Spanish joined them. A small, dark-haired woman named Mercedes flirted with him. He wanted to take her to his motel room and thought she might be willing, but when he stood, the room spun, and he felt overwhelmingly sleepy. He put his arm around her, and leaned heavily, then whispered he'd meet her here tomorrow. She helped him walk out. They laughed at what a lightweight he'd become during basic training. He kissed her sloppily when they reached her car. On the short walk back to his room he felt infused with love for his new friends.

2011

A surge of warmth and peace surged through Henry's chest as the itch on his arms and legs dissipated. He'd lived through another day in Afghanistan. As he cleaned his rifle in the dirt courtyard surrounded by mud-and-straw walls, he was immune to the stink of the latrines and his own sweat, to the sound of heavy trucks and occasional gunfire. The armored truck parked in front of the gate seemed larger than usual, the soldier inspecting it more beautiful. Sandbags and razor wire blunted his view of the jagged mountains, still snow-capped, in the distance. The pink and red poppies in the nearby fields made the austere landscape outside the gate seem almost serene. A chopper circled above raising waves of dust, then continued its inspection of the nearby hills, its noise the rhythm of his days.

Sniper shots and grenade launchers harried them daily, but whoever shot them melted into the rock. Today they'd patrolled the nearby village looking for weapons' caches and checking for improvised explosive devices. Tomorrow they'd search the poppy fields. No war on drugs here. It seemed to Henry they were protecting these fields. Henry didn't mind, glad for the hazy relief those poppies brought. Relief from his constant pain and from the long boredom interspersed with sheer terror that was his life now. Relief from the suspicion that he should have died from that IED, not kind-hearted Baxter who had a wife and three kids at home.

Anyone who'd been here a while saw each rock, each field, each child as a threat. Opium brought down the anxiety for Henry, made him able to smile at the villagers selling what produce they had. Made him able to do his job. He couldn't live believing every step he took, every road or field he cleared, could be his last. He knew he wasn't the only soldier needing this distraction, but it was against the rules, so he had to be careful. Never share. Hide it in the ground under his cot.

Henry knew his squad wouldn't leave this outpost at least until after harvest, the poppies dried, the fields cleared. Maybe then there'd be sufficient safe space that they could return to the operating base and its air conditioning and fast food and infirmaries. The last doctor he saw there refused to renew his oxy, said he didn't believe in its long-term use especially for someone as fit as Henry. But the heavy packs and guns, the repetitive landings to keep his status as a paratrooper, took their toll. He'd denied for a long time he was an addict, supplementing the pills he'd bought for cash in Florida with the prescriptions he could get after a training mission, but when the medic cut him off, he knew. He ran out of the horded pills he stashed in old prescription bottles that helped during inspections to show he wasn't using even the amount prescribed. But this doctor seemed to guess his tricks, required him to come in at longer intervals while tapering off his pills. He'd done it. He knew he had to test clean, and he had. But the pain of walking dominated his life, and he missed the sense of elation and calm. Then a soldier who called himself Buzz slipped him a packet, told him how to ingest it safely, said it would take the edge off. Said it was a quieter high, but needles were impossible to get and harder to hide.

Once his platoon left for this outpost Henry feared withdrawal and rationed his use of his remaining packets. One morning his platoon patrolled the closest village. One soldier searched the ground for IEDs while another scanned the tree line and nearby hills. Henry was a covert observer, inspecting doorways, greeting villagers, and buying food at the local market. He liked the colorful market and Afghan street food. Lamb covered in yogurt on a flat bread was far superior to the dried ready-to-eat meals that had become the outpost's staple. He gripped his weapon fiercely to keep his hands from shaking, but he couldn't stop them when he reached for a pomegranate at a stall near the far end of the market where the unlikely smell of pickles filled the air. The seller, an old man who wore a brown turban and a loose-fitting, long-sleeved shirt, touched his hand and looked at Henry with sharp eyes. When Henry apologized, fearing he'd broken some custom by touching the fruit, the man made his own hand tremor, touched Henry's hand again, and made a smoking gesture.

The villager knew.

The old man reached into a basket underneath his table and offered Henry a leaf wrapped around a small brown ball. Henry bought it, some raisins, and a pomegranate. Slipped them into his pack, offered raisins to the other men as they walked back to camp.

Some people stay on oxy for years, for life. Why is the army so weird about it? It took a lot more of this stuff to do the trick, but it was easy to find once he knew where to look. He often volunteered for village sweeps and shopping excursions. Most men avoided the village for fear of hidden terrorists in suicide vests. Everyone had heard of somebody who'd been killed or maimed, blown up by a child/old man/woman in a burqa. The young men with guns lived in the hills, but their absence didn't make anyone safe.

Sergeant Mayor noticed, first complimenting Henry on his willingness but then Henry saw a questioning wariness in his eyes. On Henry's return one afternoon the sergeant did a spot inspection, went through his gear, made him empty his pockets, and searched his pack. Luckily, Henry hadn't bought opium that day, and Sergeant Mayor left him alone after that.

BLISTERING HEAT FUELED the troops' anxiety after the elation of learning of Osama bin Laden's death in May. Henry slept fitfully to the whap of helicopters patrolling, often startled awake by illumination bombs breaking the night's dark and silence. Bare fields provided little cover, making a nighttime raid more likely. Trips to the village were discouraged, supply drops by parachute more frequent. Troop exchange delayed. Henry wanted to trust the Afghan soldiers sharing this outpost, but he didn't. Every morning the combat engineers swept the roads of the telltale mounds or disturbed mud that threatened a bomb. Over the evening meal Henry would hear about devices exploding in front of a vehicle when someone would pray a thank you for armor. Henry had been sure mission orders were imminent when a helicopter delivered Bart, a mine sniffing dog, and his handler.

An increasing wind made sand leap and skitter on the road, warning Henry's squad to hurry as they returned from a daily patrol. Soon shards of sand battered Henry's helmet and created swirling dust devils along the path. By the time they reached the outpost gate, dust obscured nearby trees and turned the air yellow.

"Dust storm!" a disembodied voice yelled from the loudspeakers. "Take cover."

The squad scattered. Soldiers took videos on their phones as the air turned orange in the late afternoon sun, holding out scarves to show the strength of the wind to disbelieving family back home. Henry ran to make sure his cot was covered tight. Dust found any opening.

The air darkened quickly, and sand found its way into Henry's nose and mouth. A shot rang out, then repetitive blasts. *What idiot is shooting in this storm?*

Alarms rang throughout the compound.

"Fuck," someone shouted. Several somebodies.

Henry rushed to his position on the wall, trained his weapon toward movement. Someone opened the gate and several soldiers rushed in, one carried by two others. A squad hadn't made it back in time, and the enemy claimed their advantage. No helicopter cover was possible in this wind and dust, and thermal radar was their only hope to see where the enemy might be.

"Drone down! We're blind here!"

As the sand enveloped and blinded them, it seemed to Henry as if he were the only person on earth despite the shouts and artillery fire. Useless. Alone. A gun in his hand but no one to shoot. No one warned him about this. The panic. The disembodied fear. The shadowy enemy. How was he to fight? No one can kill a ghost. No one can fight an evil he can't see.

An explosion. The boom of a grenade launcher. A high pitched squeal.

"Incoming!"

It felt like hours of artillery fire and grenades condensed into a timeless fog. Henry thought he saw rats scurrying back behind the rocks and tree line, heard the whap of helicopter rotors in the distance as the darkness thinned, the sun low in the sky.

Two bearded bodies lay in the road. Too close.

"Stand down!"

Henry slid toward a clutch of men and allowed himself to be hugged. Kissed Sergeant Mayor's helmet.

"Don't get all gay on me, Canuck," Sergeant Mayor said, punching Henry on the shoulder.

Henry could barely hear for the roar in his head. Two men with a litter carrying a bloody man ran toward the trauma tent. A medic kneeled in front of a blasted wall and carefully removed the body armor of a soldier lying on the ground. Several craters littered the courtyard.

Nowhere was safe.

A medivac landed. It left loaded with screaming soldiers and some not screaming.

Henry lay on his cot, a pinch of his brown paste curled on his tongue. As he waited for his dread to lessen, blasts sounded in his head. After a half hour he took a pinch more and slept fitfully.

An alarm in the night. A whizzing sound in the distance. An explosion nearby.

A pinch more.

Ricky, who slept on the other side of Henry's canvas room, yelled, "Canuck, aren't you getting up. Come on, man."

Now Ricky was shaking him. "I know what you do. But you can't let them see it."

Henry knew this. He didn't care but sat up anyway.

"Put on your sunglasses," Ricky said as they walked toward breakfast. "Sit there." He pointed to a chair outside the mess hall. "I'll bring some food."

In the courtyard stood three pairs of boots, three helmets, and three dog tags atop three rifles in front of an American flag. The bodies were on their way home. Henry stood in front of each, head bent, before reading the dog tags. He knew them. Martin Talsen, an engineer from Michigan. Cory Adanz, a Marine from Utah. Hana Wal, a medic from Hawaii. *Why can't I cry?* All he felt was empty. *It should have been me.*

"There'll be a service later," Ricky said, standing next to Henry and handing him a cup of coffee.

Sergeant Mayor stood next to them. "Sad day."

Henry swayed a little as he nodded. The sergeant watched him stumble back to his chair, then looked at Ricky with a question in his eyes.

A WEEK AFTER the memorial, when life had more or less gotten back to normal, Sergeant Mayor called Henry in for a drug test.

He failed.

"You need help, Canuck," Sergeant Mayor said. "And I'm going to make sure you get it. I'll contact Base. I'm sending you back on the next helicopter and recommending you for the Army's Substance Abuse Program."

Henry nodded. There was no point in arguing.

The base doctor who'd weaned him off oxy met him at the helipad and took Henry to Military Police.

"I got him clean before he left," the doctor said. "Looks like a rehabilitation failure to me."

Henry told them about his injuries and how he needed supplements for his pain. For days, the police badgered him about where he got his supply, interfered in his detox, played on his agitation. Let him sweat. He told them about Buzz, but no one knew a soldier with that name and the MPs decided he was lying. Told him buying from a villager was the same as funding the Taliban. Arrested him, swabbed his cheek, grilled him for hours.

After the first week, Henry's only human contacts were a psychologist who came to check off boxes on his sheet of paper, a medic, his judge advocate, and an array of officers whose sole purpose seemed to be to berate him. He didn't know if anyone tried to visit. He only knew he was alone. His judge advocate tried to explain what was happening, but Henry didn't care. He knew what he did was wrong but didn't know how he could have done anything different. He needed to numb the pain to do his job, to survive. The Army gave him oxy then took it away.

"I admit I took the drugs," Henry said, begging to be placed in a civilian rehabilitation program, not discharged. "I don't want to be one of those junkies I saw in Florida."

Henry's judge advocate pushed for a reduction in the charges to allow an administrative separation, but the commander resisted. Wanted to set an example for the troops. Henry's advocate argued the drug use was directly related to injuries received as a part of his service, and Henry should have access to medical benefits.

Three months later, the Army was still arguing about what should be done. Henry was clean, but his pain returned worse than he remembered. And his nightmares intensified. Explosions surrounded him every day and night, real and imagined. Helicopters passed overhead constantly. The days and nights merged into indistinguishable bursts of pain and noise and isolation. He feared he'd never be free. When the Army proposed a General Discharge and said he could receive VA medical benefits, he said yes immediately.

TWO SHOTS ECHOED in the predawn silence. Traveler raised his head from the river water and strained his ears in their direction. A smell of fear accompanied the sounds of breaking twigs, a quick yell then a whimper, and the thump of feet coming closer, then veering back into the denser forest. Another shot, the sound of a body dropping, human voices. Hunters meant food, sometimes only blood, but sometimes the entrails they left behind.

Traveler trotted toward the sounds, now muffled by the rushing water echoing off the surrounding mountains and the wind carrying smells and sounds away. He slunk behind a fallen log when the sound of voices rose and he glimpsed two men covering their prey.

Traveler stayed hidden in the trees as he circled the two kneeling men. He smelled blood and a residue of fear, heard the men's gloating voices. He hoped they'd leave something for him.

Tired and hungry, Traveler ventured too close and one of the men saw him.

"Get away, you mangy mutt," the man yelled, then picked up a rock and threw it in his direction.

"I wonder what his jerky would taste like," the other man said. He took a long stick and pointed it toward Traveler.

The men lifted the body and carried it away through the trees, leaving only a trail of blood. When he no longer heard their crashing steps, Traveler lapped the blood where the body had lain, first from the grass then from the broken red heel in its midst.

SEVEN

"HOW'D SATURDAY'S SEARCH go?" Connor asked as Officer Sweka and a red-bearded tech from the County's IT department crouched over a computer keyboard, trying to sharpen the casino's security tapes. The three of them crowded into Connor's office, window blinds shut tight and door closed. Connor loosened his tie and took off his jacket. Sweka had removed his hat and placed it on the credenza, but kept his uniform buttoned.

"We didn't find anything. I'm glad. I hope she left town and one day Therese will get a call." Sweka kept his eye on the computer monitor. "Layla and I went through these security tapes yesterday and tried to match it to our list of who was invited to the Memorial Day Party." He handed a copy of the list to Connor.

"This is great." Connor recognized a few names from the list, surprised to see his elderly neighbors, a few county employees, and a local lawyer on the list.

"Hey Tom," Connor said to the tech. "We're going to need to have screen grabs of every face we can. Can you do that while we watch? The more we get identified today the better off we are."

"Sure, but we might be here all day. How fast you want this to run?" Tom asked, scratching his beard. "We've got tapes from two room cameras and two exit cameras."

"Are they time stamped?"

"Yep."

"Can we run the room cameras side by side?"

Tom sighed. "Yes, but I'll need another laptop and projector. Be right back."

"Let's divvy up the interviews with who we know was there," Connor said as he took down framed diplomas to create a bare white wall. "I'll do Mr. Kam. The sheriff says he's a shady guy, but from what Ms. Flynn told me he looks pretty central."

"I know all the Casino employees, so I'll talk with them and invite you to a real interview if it seems like they saw something," Sweka said.

Connor nodded. Too many people at this party to do much more initially than informal interviews. Everyone might be a suspect, but they had to focus the work somehow. "Galmenberg Police said they're going around Diyanni's neighborhood this week, see if anyone saw her or if she shows up on any security video after Memorial Day. It looks like she doesn't have any bank accounts or credit cards. Did everything with cash I guess."

Tom returned and set up the second laptop and projector, then synced the timestamps on two recordings as they shone against the wall. They spent the next several hours watching the videos, making a picture index, identifying who they could, deciding who they wanted to interview first.

At noon they had a greasy pizza delivered and kept watching.

The videos were decent quality, but most of the cameras were mounted high and pitched so that the facial features of the moving partiers were difficult to distinguish. Tom increased the size when they asked, but that just made them blurrier. Connor knew he would need to go through the tapes again on a smaller screen, a frame at a time. *The BIA or FBI should be doing this,* he grumbled to himself.

Maybe the woman did just leave to start a new life, Connor thought as the hours dragged on. Some people did. But it nagged at him. Diyanni'd never contacted her mom or boyfriend, took nothing with her. No, there was a bad ending here, he was sure of it.

When they'd finally finished the party room tapes, Connor decided it was enough for the day. "The last time we saw her in the party room was 11:53," he said and Sweka agreed. "You've been through all these tapes three times now and don't see her leaving the building in any of them."

"I'm a little concerned about that group in the far parking lot at 12:10," Sweka said. "But it's too dark to see any faces or license plates."

"I can try to clean that up," Tom said. "But I'm not hopeful."

Connor nodded. "Tom, could you create two files, one with identified and the other with unidentified faces?"

"Easy peasy," Tom said. "It's done and on its way."

"Can we get facial recognition software to identify the ones we couldn't?" The images were grainy, but it was worth a try.

"Sure, but the best comparison database is drivers' licenses and the Department of Licensing makes us get a warrant before it will let us use its database," Tom said. "Get one, and we'll do it for you."

Connor frowned. *Facebook identifies people on my pictures all the time*. "Well, we've divvied up a pretty long list of people to contact," Connor said to Sweka as he was leaving. "It's a start."

Sweka nodded. "My fellow officers will help."

"Are you aware of any similar cases?"

"Depends on what you mean by similar," Sweka said. "I've seen lots of reports about missing Indigenous women."

Connor nodded. "I've found several reports of missing young women on state patrol's database, mostly runaway teenagers. A couple of women have been reported missing after large events like yours. Locally, we have several open cases from the last few years that don't seem similar. A woman who supposedly had been living in the forest who her friend says is missing, a prostitute last seen at a bar in Galmenberg. We get reports about missing women pretty regularly from other jurisdictions, but don't do much other than keep an eye out."

"Canada's got a task force," Sweka said. "We should have one too."

"One of our attorneys said the same thing. Let's start one here," Connor said. "State patrol has a missing and unidentified persons unit. I'll contact them. See if they have any leads or have seen any patterns."

Sweka shook Connor's hand as he left.

Connor wondered if he should ask Deputy Springer to do some of the interviews. He wasn't sure how good Springer would be at getting information from people who'd been at what they thought was a private party. The sheriff had called Springer impolitic, after all. Instead, Connor telephoned Kelly.

"We need more to get a warrant to use Licensing's database," Kelly said. "The judge will probably call it a fishing expedition and deny it, but I can try. Send your unidentified ones over to me. I'll see if I recognize anyone while I prepare the affidavit."

"If you can identify a few more, great. We need some leads."

"I'll see what I can come up with and send you a draft," Kelly said. "Somebody at that party's got to know something."

THE NEXT MORNING Connor took advantage of the rare sunny day and walked the few short blocks from the sheriff's department to Mr. Kam's office. He preferred to visit witnesses unannounced, believing an element of surprise always helped get to the truth. The office complex was a squat five-story concrete structure with narrow windows built during the early sixties. He wondered why anyone ever thought its brutalist style of architecture was a good idea. Inside, the lobby smelled musty, and its humming fluorescent lights threw cold light on its gray cement floors. Prickles of sweat formed on his face and arms as he waited for the elevator in the dank room.

The elevator arrived with a thud and its heavy door ground open. It crept upward, marking each floor with a creak and a clunk, finally opening to worn beige carpeting in a silent hallway lined with closed doors. Kam, Inc. was the third door on the left and had an intercom next to its locked door. Connor pressed its sticky button, and he heard a buzz behind the door. When no one answered, he tried again.

"Yes?" a soft voice said.

"Hi, I'm here to see Mr. Kam?" Connor said.

"Do you have an appointment?" the voice asked.

"No, I'm Detective Andino from the Cascadia County Sheriff's Office. I just need to ask him a couple of questions about one of his employees."

The silence lasted for over a minute, so Connor pushed the button again. This time, a dark-haired woman dressed in a vibrant red and yellow flowered dress opened the door. A lacquered black desk in front of four tall filing cabinets filled the small reception area. Two plastic chairs sat along a blank wall broken by two steel doors. The whine of the ceiling lights was even louder here, and several were burned out. The woman pointed to a short man now standing in one of the doorways.

The man's face shifted from irritation to one of false welcome. "Detective Andino, to what do I owe the pleasure?"

"Mr. Kam?"

"Yes, sorry, I'm Oliver Kam." He grasped Connor's hand with a crushing shake. "How can I help you?"

"Diyanni Hupt's mom has reported her missing, and it seems the last time anyone saw her was with you at a Memorial Day party at the Nininpak Casino."

"Come in, sit down," Kam said, waving Connor into his office, then closing the door.

Kam sat in a large chair behind an enormous desk, his head framed in the daylight of the first unshaded window Connor had seen since entering the building. The glare tempted him to look away, but he figured this was a power play and focused instead on Kam's shadowed face.

"Diyanni's young, flighty, not very dependable. We gave her a chance by bringing her to that party, and then she left with someone else. We had to fire her," Kam said, rocking a little in his chair.

"Did you see who she left with?"

"No, she must have snuck out around midnight when lots of people were leaving and staff was cleaning up. I rounded up the other girls who'd come with me about that time, but we couldn't find Diyanni. My wife checked the bathrooms, asked the other servers, but she wasn't anywhere. So we left. What else could we do?"

Connor didn't trust Kam but sensed he was telling the truth even if he were leaving something out.

"Has this ever happened before?" Connor asked.

"Never. I watch out for my girls."

"Ever heard of anyone else going missing after a party?"

Kam leaned back in his chair and closed his eyes. After a few seconds he opened them. "No."

Connor stood. He was pretty sure that was a lie. *What is he hiding?*

"Thank you for your time," Connor said as he left. When he had more, he'd do an interrogation.

EIGHT

THE NIGHT OF the prosecuting attorney's public forum was blustery, and the clouds threatened more rain. Kelly bent her head against the wind, distracted with her usual presentation jitters. She stopped short when she heard her name, inches away from a local attorney, Maury Topper, on the sidewalk leading to the County Commission Chambers. She apologized, and he laughed, asked how things were going. She'd seen his name on the list for the Casino's Memorial Day party Connor sent over, so asked him what he remembered.

"The police asked me that too," Maury said. "Not much. It was a fun party. Good food, lots of alcohol. I went with some buddies and we laughed a lot and flirted with the women."

"Do you remember the server in a red dress?"

"Sure. Pretty, young. Is she still missing?"

Kelly nodded.

"We gave her a couple of good tips so she came around a fair amount. We stayed until the fireworks then went to play poker at my friend Stan's house."

"What time was that?

"Around ten-thirty. How are you involved?"

"I met her mom and said I'd do what I could. This is breaking her heart."

"I bet." A worried frown crossed Maury's face. "I'll keep trying to remember, talk with my buddies. But don't get your hopes up."

Kelly shook her head. What hopes?

"So this thing tonight," Maury said. "Will we get CLE credit?"

"Sadly, no," Kelly said. "It's geared to a general audience."

"Well, I'm here. I might as well stay."

Once the group settled into their seats in the auditorium, Kelly introduced Prosecuting Attorney Paltik. She emphasized his education, his awards, and his ongoing service to the community. Paltik talked about the structure of the office and how although his title was "Prosecuting Attorney" he also represented the county in civil matters. He stressed the importance of the rule of law in the prevention of tyranny of both the government and mob rule. The committee had allotted him twenty minutes, but Kelly wasn't going to say anything when his talk went past time and veered toward a law and order speech.

Paltik had, after all the committee's discussions, nixed all their proposals and directed them to talk about freedom under the law. He was probably right, seeing how he'd picked a day right between Juneteenth and the Fourth of July. He wanted them to discuss how laws bring order to society so we can live peacefully together and avoid the kind of attitudes that led to societal crimes. How the freedoms promised by the Bill of Rights prevented the government from overreaching. Kelly could think of a lot of examples where that hadn't worked so well, but Paltik wanted to talk about the promise of the shining city on the hill more than the sometimes dark reality. And she wanted to believe in that too. Well, maybe the arc of history did bend toward justice. She hoped it did.

Tonight's meeting would focus on what many residents thought were overreaching government regulations, a favorite campaign topic. Kelly contacted the state ombudsmen and discovered citizens complained most about their neighbors, contractors, and employers. Since they knew those topics were way too broad for an evening meeting, Kelly, Clara, and Dave each took a category and decided on small discussion groups to debate a specific polarizing law, who might be the victims, and how strenuously they should be prosecuted.

After Paltik finished, a few reporters tried to ask questions about a pending criminal case against a state legislator. He waved them off, saying that was better discussed at a different forum.

Clara took the podium next, and her genius as a litigator shone in her assured posture and engaging smile. People who had been starting to nod sat straighter. "Why do we need so many laws?" she asked, and sounds of agreement peppered the room. "And why, when you need the law's help, is it so hard to get?"

Kelly thought she heard someone say "Amen."

"I went to law school with those questions firmly in mind," Clara continued. "I married young and soon discovered I'd made a mistake. A big mistake. We'll leave it at that." A few laughs erupted. "It was easy to get married, but hard to get a divorce. I didn't have the money to hire a lawyer, so pulled out the statute figuring I was smart enough to do this myself." She paused. "I was not. My case didn't even start at first because my ex wasn't home when the process server showed up. How many here would know what to do next?" A few hands raised, including Maury Topper. "Lawyers don't count, Maury. Then, once it was filed, the judge threw my case out for failing to follow statutory requirements I hadn't understood. After the hearing, a kind attorney sitting in the back took me aside and told me how to fix it. I'll never forget my astonishment. My ideas and intent were spot on, but I'd used the wrong words. I went to law school partly to never feel that helpless again and partly to try to fix the system to make it easier for the next gal."

One person in the back clapped. Clara gave her brightest smile.

"What we're going to try to do tonight is take some of the mystery out of laws that affect everyone. No one wants to be told what to do, but you'd be surprised how many people want to tell other people what to do. I want to take a helicopter to work and land it on my roof, but my neighbors aren't keen. There's a law for that. I'm afraid vaccines harm children and won't give them to mine, but if I don't the school won't let my kids in. There's a law for that. Companies for years dumped toxic waste, people dumped their sewage, into lakes and rivers and people got sick. There are laws for that, hard as they might be to enforce." Clara turned to Dave, who replaced her at the podium.

"Clara's point, if it's not obvious already," Dave said, "is a restriction for one person or group is intended to be freeing or helpful for another. A neighbor free from helicopter noise, children protected from measles, a reduction in cancer and food poisoning. But when do the laws go too far?" He paused and looked around the room. "To focus our discussion tonight, you've been given a handout with three statutes and a related county ordinance for each. One is the establishment of a minimum wage, another is the law requiring licensing of contractors, and the third is the prohibition of short term rentals in residential neighborhoods. We think small groups will give everyone a chance to express their opinions which we will document and give to the prosecuting attorney. Clara, Kelly, and I will moderate small groups on each of these topics. Let's take a break, drink some coffee, and come back in ten minutes where you can choose the group that interests, or enrages, you the most."

The volume of conversations grew as people went to the back for coffee or to the restrooms. Kelly knew many would leave, not interested in sharing their opinions with others, and those that stayed would have strong opinions. She didn't mind. She liked a good debate. Paltik left as discreetly as possible, but everyone noticed, and the reporters followed him out.

Kelly joined the coffee line behind Maury Topper.

"Which group are you leading?" Maury asked.

"Party houses—the short term rental group," she said.

"That's the one I'm interested in. I represent some companies with several short term rental properties," Maury said.

"Good! I'm guessing most people in the group will be opposed to them," she said.

"While Paltik was talking, I thought about that Memorial Day party," Maury said. "I do remember a guy who kept going up to the servers when they were by themselves. I think I saw him talking to the girl in the red dress on the upstairs patio. I thought at the time he was looking for a pickup, got the sense they were all turning him down."

"Would you recognize him if you saw his picture?"

"I don't know. It was over six weeks ago and pictures aren't the same as seeing someone walking around."

"The Casino has security video."

"That might work."

"If you're willing to have a look, I'll let the detectives know."

"Sure. Anything to help."

THE DARK SKY told Kelly it was late, at least nine-thirty. She glanced at her phone. Yes, almost ten. She called Ruth's cell, but she didn't answer. *Where is she?* Ruth hadn't said anything about going out during their quick supper of leftover lasagna, one of many pre-made meals Kelly cooked on the weekend to reheat during the week. She had stopped herself from asking Ruth what she'd be doing that night as she was trying hard to give Ruth space, show Ruth she trusted her. *Maybe she has her headphones on. Or left her phone in her backpack.* Kelly smirked at that thought. *She's probably texting someone and can't be bothered.*

Lights shone throughout the house when Kelly pulled into the driveway a half hour later, but only Babs greeted her with a long meow. Kelly poured a glass of wine from the refrigerator, wrinkling her nose at its vinegary taste as she looked around downstairs. She trudged up to Ruth's bedroom, knocked lightly, then opened the door a crack. No Ruth. She resisted the need to text her. She'd wait, watch the news for the half hour until Ruth's curfew.

The cheerful newsreaders on the local station kept Kelly's anxiety at bay with sports scores and weather reports mixed between political ads. At eleven, Kelly decided to give Ruth fifteen minutes leeway. Those minutes dragged by. Kelly emptied the dishwasher, brought out the garbage. 11:07. She folded the towels left in the dryer and put them away. 11:10. Added to her grocery list. 11:11. Broke down shipping boxes that had accumulated and put them in the recycling bin. 11:13. Then she paced, her anxiety and anger increasing with every step.

At 11:15 she texted: "Where are you?"

An agonizing minute, later Ruth responded: "home soon how was ur meeting"

"OK. Should I come get you?"

"no im good"

Five minutes later, the heavy motor of the garage door started and stopped then started again. Kelly opened the door between the house and the garage and simmered as Ruth lifted her bike onto its wall hooks. They glared at each other over the trunk of Kelly's car.

"You're late," Kelly said. "Where were you? You didn't say you were going anywhere."

"I wasn't going to, and you weren't here to tell."

"You could have texted or left a note."

"I figured I'd be back before you were."

"I need to know you're safe!" Kelly's skin prickled and her stomach roiled. She hated yelling but didn't know how to get through to Ruth.

"Here I am," Ruth said. "Can you get out of the doorway?"

Kelly moved aside. "Just tell when you're going to be late, OK?"

Ruth shrugged, picked Babs up, climbed the stairs, and slammed the door to her room.

NINE

CONNOR CLOSED HIS office door to muffle the din of ringing telephones and loud but indistinguishable conversations. Before he reached his desk, a quick knock and rush of noise announced Sheriff Nisser.

"Got a call from the FBI this morning," Sheriff Nisser said.

Connor smiled hopefully. Maybe they were finally interested in his case.

"Missing college girl at UW supposedly came up to Galmenberg for the Fourth of July weekend and never returned to her dorm. Skipped classes yesterday. Her parents say it's not like her."

"Why the FBI? Seems like state patrol or Seattle police would take it."

Nisser shrugged and handed Connor a slip of paper. "I guess patrol asked for help. Not sure why. Give the agent a call."

The sheriff's note contained only a DC telephone number, and two names: Agent Patrick Carter and Hannah Vandaroot. Intrigued, Connor did a quick internet search and scrolled through several Seattle news stories from this morning, all of which showed a smiling blonde in a high school sports uniform holding a volleyball. Hannah was a sophomore honors student from Minnesota, her dad a local politician. Last Thursday night she headed north to Galmenberg with a guy she'd just met. Hannah's parents called on Sunday to find her gone, then called her roommate again on Monday before calling Seattle police. She'd now been gone three days. Six if you count back to Friday.

Three days. And the FBI was already involved. Connor shook his head. Did her being a college student make her less of an adult than Diyanni? No, the dad must have well-connected friends. Connor wondered whether he should call Seattle police first. Maybe they'd talked to Galmenberg police. Well, he could push Diyanni's case when he talked to the agent about Hannah, now that he had a name and an excuse to call.

Agent Carter spoke quickly when Connor reached him, asked Connor to coordinate with state patrol. Said he'd be coming out to Washington if there was evidence of foul play or an extended absence.

"Glad to help," Connor said. "I have another case that should interest you, too. A missing Nininpak woman. I've been trying to work through the

Bureau of Indian Affairs, but haven't had much luck. She's been missing almost three months now. We could use some help."

"Is she in the database?" Carter asked.

"Yes. Diyanni Hupt."

Keyboard taps and a long silence followed.

"What kind of help do you need?"

Connor explained what he knew about Diyanni's disappearance, how the only lead was a party with several hundred people. "Interviews are our first priority. We need to figure out who many of the people at the party are and who she left the party with. Then follow-ups and background checks and reviewing security tapes near her house and work, checking for similar cases. Pretty labor intensive, as you know."

"Any ground searches?"

"The Tribe has organized searches around the Casino and on the Reservation, but honestly we don't know where to start looking."

"I'll have the local agent-in-charge give you a call," Carter said and hung up.

Connor hoped that was true. The phone rang.

"Your eleven o'clock interview is here," the desk sergeant said.

Connor grabbed his suit jacket from the hook on his door, pulled his tie tighter, and combed his hair with his fingers. He'd intended to prep more for this interview, but he couldn't very well send her home. He grabbed Diyanni's file, a pad of yellow lined paper, and two pens.

As he neared the front desk, Connor assessed the young woman standing in the waiting area. She had long, dark hair tied near her neck and wore a snug lace shirt over black yoga pants and flip flops on her pale feet with purple nail polish. Her stance was rigid and her arms crossed. Not a willing witness, then.

Connor held the door open and stood in the doorway. "Kyrsten, thank you so much for coming in." He gave her his warmest smile, and she seemed to thaw. "We could use your help."

"I hope this doesn't take too long," Kyrsten said. "I have work this afternoon."

"As quick as we can," Connor said. "I'll show you a few pictures and a short bit of video. Shouldn't take too long."

Kyrsten nodded and came through the door in a whiff of stale smoke. She followed him into a small room where Tom the IT tech sat with an open laptop.

"Kyrsten, this is Tom." Tom lifted his head from staring at the laptop and gave a little wave. "He'll be showing you the pictures. But first, let's go over what you told me on the phone. You were working the Casino party on Memorial Day, and a man approached you and asked if you'd be willing to work at his after-party, am I correct?"

"Yes."

"But you said no?"

"Yes. I didn't know him."

"Describe him for me again. This is important, so I want Tom to hear it from you."

"OK. He was an older white guy, medium height, maybe five ten or eleven."

"So, six or seven inches taller than you?"

"Yeah. He had longish gray hair, curly on the ends. I thought it might be a wig."

"A wig? Why did you think that?"

"I don't know. I just did. Some guys are embarrassed about their hair. Or lack of it."

"But you're not sure."

"No, it was just a sense I had."

"What else. His build, his clothes?"

"Long sleeve dark blue shirt, dark pants, blue or black, I can't remember. Loose fitting, so I'd say he was on the thin side, but I have no idea if he was muscular, he wasn't fat. He was ordinary. Nothing flashy."

"Any distinguishing features?"

"His hair was unusual, like I said. So if he wasn't wearing it or cut it I might not recognize him. Oh, and his hands looked rough, like he worked with his hands. A mechanic or a farmer, maybe."

"Thank you, Kyrsten. This is very helpful. We have photos and clips from the party's security tapes, and we'd like to know if any of these men could be the man who asked you to the after-party."

Kyrsten nodded.

Tom turned the laptop toward Kyrsten. "I've pulled out the men with gray hair. Let's look at those first."

One by one, Kyrsten looked, then shook her head.

"OK," Tom said. "Here are the guys in dark blue long sleeve shirts, in case he was wearing a wig."

Again, Kyrsten shook her head at each screen shot.

"You're doing great," Connor said. "We have a few group pictures for you to look through, just in case."

On the third screen shot, Kyrsten pointed to a man almost outside the camera angle. "Maybe him. I can't see his face."

"We couldn't either," Connor said. "Whoever this is was careful about staying in the crowd and looking away from the cameras."

"Sorry I couldn't be more help," Kyrsten said.

"No need to be sorry. The more people we can eliminate, the better. Thank you," Connor said. "I'll walk you out."

CONNOR NEEDED TO eat before all the caffeine he'd been drinking made him too shaky to think straight. He needed to call Officer Sweka and tell him about Krysten and the FBI. He needed to talk to Detective Olafson at Galmenberg Police. He needed to talk with Kelly. He needed to at least read through all the new files in his in box.

But he needed to eat more. He'd ask Olafson to meet over lunch.

"Sure," Detective Olafson said. "How about Sherry's Kitchen, right next to the Galmenberg station, in a half hour? I'm not much of a walker these days."

Sherry's Kitchen reminded Connor of a Cracker Barrel without the rockers or the store. Country kitchen style, with the comforting smell of fried chicken and meatloaf filling the room. Plates and tin coffee pots and iron pots filled shelves around the room and pictures of roosters and sunflowers covered the walls. He'd never met Olafson, but Deputy Springer had told him to expect a large, older man. Connor decided the white-haired man lumbering past the big front window toward the door must be him, so he waved when the man entered.

"Are you Detective Olafson?"

"Call me John," the man said and thrust his beefy hand forward. "But yes."

"I'm Connor Andino."

"It's good to finally meet you," Olafson said, catching his breath.

Connor wondered how long it had been since Olafson had been in patrol. Or climbed some stairs. The sleeves of his shirt stretched like sausage casings and his stomach fell over his belt when he sat. A glistening drop of sweat hovered near the earpiece of his glasses, waiting to drop. Connor told himself not to judge. Springer said he was brilliant and generous with his time and insights. *A genius,* Springer told him. *With a mind as limber as his body used to be.*

Connor asked to sit in a booth away from the other diners.

"Don't worry," Olafson said. "I don't see any reporters in here."

"I did want to talk to you about a couple of cases. I got a call to look for a Hannah Vandaroot and I think we're both looking for Diyanni Hupt."

A second of confusion flashed in Olafson's face. "Yes. We're pretty focused on Hannah right now. Not much going on with Diyanni."

Connor stifled a grimace. "What do you have on Hannah? Where was she going up here? Any sightings?"

"State patrol thinks she and the guy she was with were going camping, so I told them you should be involved. They bought gas and junk food on her daddy's credit card at the downtown Quick Mart. I'll email you the security video. Decent pictures of both of them, but I didn't see any camping gear. Could have been in the trunk. We've sent the pictures to all the hotels and motels in Galmenberg and nearby, but nobody's recognized them yet. We're going on the news tonight if you want to be there. Sheriff says he's coming. We'll do a call for leads and search volunteers."

Connor nodded, hoping they get better information and more volunteers than they had with Diyanni. "We'll get some patrol officers to check the usual camping places, but if they were wilderness camping, they could be anywhere."

Connor looked longingly at Olafson's meat loaf and mashed potatoes when their orders arrived as he tried to convince himself his grilled fish was better. A heavy lunch always made him sleepy in the afternoon. "I know you're busy, but we could use some help with Diyanni's case too. Could we set up a group meeting to share information? No point duplicating work."

Olafson stared at him with piercing ice blue eyes. "The last thing any of us needs is another meeting."

"I hear you," Connor said. "But we've got to coordinate too. On all these cases."

Olafson put his knife and fork on the edge of his plate. "Maybe you don't understand how small our department is. Special Victims? That's me. Missing Persons? That's me. Homicide? One detective and one floater who also works with Drug Investigations. And me if needed. County has twice as many deputies. You know who should be working on Diyanni's case? The feds. I can't help it if they're not."

"I did bring it up with the agent this morning."

"Good. But in my experience, don't hold your breath."

They concentrated on their food, then asked for separate checks.

"So, you're not interested in coordinating," Connor said.

"I didn't say that," Olafson said as he withdrew cash from his wallet. "Of course we should keep each other informed. When I get back to my office, I'll send you what I have on Hannah and Diyanni. But no meetings or task forces or whatever you want to call them, at least not right now. Try me again in a couple of months. Or when we find Hannah."

TEN

KELLY'S PHONE DINGED as she sat at her desk reading police reports and drinking cold coffee. An email from Connor. She fought her disappointment when she saw the email contained an attachment but no text. She'd thought he was interested. She'd left him a voice mail about Maury. *And his response is a case status memo telling me he interviewed a bunch of people and had no more leads?*

Kelly didn't know if Therese had created an email account and was sure Connor didn't have it, so she called. Therese answered on the first ring. Officer Sweka had brought a copy of the memo to her. Therese had lots of questions that neither Officer Sweka nor Kelly could answer. "I want to hear what Detective Andino has to say. Can you come if he'll meet?"

"Sure," Kelly said. "How about I set something up so it works with my schedule?"

Connor was abrupt with Kelly when he answered and set up the meeting, but the next day he was cheerful and welcoming when he joined her, Therese, and Daniel Sweka at the police station in a small room crowded with a metal table and four stackable chairs.

"We contacted the FBI again," Sweka said. "They still don't seem particularly interested. They and Galmenberg are all caught up in this Hannah Vandaroot case."

"I feel sad for her parents," Therese said. "I hope they find her."

Kelly's stomach clenched, and she stifled a frown. Hannah's case had made national news for three nights in a row now, all showing a crying mother and an angry father. She felt terribly for Hannah's parents, worried about Ruth, but it aggravated her that Diyanni's case never got that kind of attention. One station used Hannah as a way to criticize dating sites, another stood on the lawn near Hannah's dorm asking young women if they were scared. "Of course they are!" she'd yelled at the television, causing Ruth to roll her eyes and leave the room.

"Me too," Sweka said. "Therese, you were at all of our woodland searches and know they turned up nothing. Layla brought in Mr. Kam. He provides services to our hotel, so decided to be helpful, gave us his guest list. Said they were all fine, upstanding citizens and they've never had any problems. Hinted that Diyanni wasn't a reliable worker which is why he didn't think much about her not leaving with them that night. Figured she'd left early."

Therese bristled, but said nothing. Kelly pushed up her glasses then crossed her arms.

"I talked with Maury Topper, one of the guys I recognized on the tapes. Did you follow up with him?" Kelly asked.

Connor ruffled through his file. "Yep. Not much there. For one, he has dark hair. And he left with a group of people about ten-thirty after the fireworks and spent the next couple of hours playing poker at one of their houses. Their alibis for that night are solid. He's coming in next week to look at the tapes."

"We talked to several of the men at the party who are regulars at the casino," Sweka continued. "They remembered talking with Dee, said she was nice, pretty, had a great laugh. None noticed anything out of the ordinary. A couple said they'd probably drunk too much and didn't remember much after about eleven p.m. One did give us the name of one of the men we saw talking with Diyanni on the tape." Sweka looked at his notes. "Tom Barnes. Galmenberg police followed up with him."

"We did background checks on everybody identified from the tapes and guest lists, including Mr. Barnes," Connor said. "And Mr. Topper. There's a pretty broad mix of businessmen, farmers, young, old. No sex offenders. They all said they remembered Diyanni but didn't see anything unusual. No one remembers being invited to an after-party. Then we interviewed all the servers, asked them if they'd been approached. Two of the servers said they'd been invited to after parties but not for money, and they declined to go. We showed them our screen shots of men at the party, but they couldn't say which one."

"Maury said he saw a guy approach several servers."

Connor shrugged. "Hopefully Mr. Topper can point that guy out. Pinny tried to describe the man Diyanni'd pointed out to her. Said he had salt-and-pepper hair and wore jeans and a dark collared shirt-which describes over half the men we saw on the tape, but said she never got a good look at him. She couldn't pick him out from our photos either."

"Layla and I went through the tapes again and got face shots of all the men with gray hair," Sweka said. "Pinny eliminated a couple, but that left thirty to consider. One of the servers said she remembered a small group leaving a side exit around midnight but she didn't see anyone in a red dress with them. We checked the tapes again and saw a small group leaving around the same time. We didn't catch any good face shots, though, and no red dresses. They walked into a dark part of the parking lot so we didn't see them after that."

Sweka paused to speak directly to Therese. "Most of these guys are regulars and we've had no trouble or reports with them before. We had no reports of disturbance in the parking lot that night either. I believe whatever happened with Dee didn't happen at the Casino."

"It is looking that way," Connor said.

"Could someone uninvited have gotten in?" Kelly asked.

"Probably," Sweka said. "Especially if someone invited let that person in through one of the kitchen or back doors."

"Our media appeals led to a number of reported sightings," Connor said. "Nothing's panned out so far. Therese, we do have some video from stores where citizens say they saw Diyanni. We'd like you to look at them to see if you recognize her. Do you have time for that today?"

Hopefulness shone from Therese's body. "Yes. Daniel, can you look with me and take me home?"

Daniel took her hand. "Of course."

Kelly felt helpless, useless, not sure why she was even here. Guilt about the files piling on her desk washed over her. She wanted to help, but wanting to and actually helping weren't the same thing. She stood up to leave.

"Thank you, Kelly," Therese said with hesitation in her voice and in her soft touch on Kelly's arm. "Your support means a lot."

Kelly smiled. "Any time."

Connor walked with Kelly to the parking lot. "Sorry I didn't get back to you about Mr. Topper. Things have been crazy with all the attention being paid to Hannah Vandaroot. I meant to call."

Kelly felt her body relax. "It's OK. I know I'm not really on the investigative team."

"I meant, well," Connor said, then paused. "How about we meet for a beer sometime?"

"I'd like that."

"I'll call you."

Maybe he will, maybe he won't.

KELLY WAITED A week for Connor to call before deciding he wouldn't, a week where the news about Hannah Vandaroot had been relegated to the middle of local news broadcasts and most days didn't make the national news. Kelly saw Mr. Vandaroot in Paltik's office one afternoon, and his shouts if not his words could be heard in the lobby. She wondered what would happen if Therese tried something that confrontational. *Probably still nothing.* It wasn't Therese's style anyway.

The next week, Hannah's face shone from the morning newspaper once again. "Please respect our privacy," the article quoted her dad as saying. "We're just glad she's back." Every day a little more of the story came out. Hannah on a rafting trip away from cell phone service, eventually arrested for driving under the influence in Boise, her date for possession of a controlled substance. She'd missed too many classes to stay in summer school. "We're taking her home," the dad said.

Kelly thought about giving the article to Ruth, but figured she'd see it on her own. Things had been relatively peaceful at home this week. *I need to resist my need to make this a cautionary tale.*

Kelly was scanning her email when her phone rang. A notification on her computer said it was from the sheriff's office.

"Would you like to be part of a task force addressing the problem of missing women?" Connor asked.

"I didn't know there was one," Kelly said.

"There isn't, yet. I think we need one, and with this Vandaroot case the sheriff and Galmenberg police think so too. It'd be good to have legal counsel involved. Or at least available for questions. Is that something your boss would authorize?"

"I think so," Kelly said. "Who's on it?"

"Well, to start, you, me, and Daniel Sweka from the Nininpak Police Force. Olafson from Galmenberg Police said he'd help when he could, but he, and I quote, wasn't interested in going to a bunch of meetings Anyone else you can think of?"

"I'll talk to the prosecuting attorney. He might want to be the one involved."

"Right, election year." The scowl in Connor's voice made Kelly repress a laugh.

"I'm sure he'll delegate."

"It'll be pretty informal for now," Connor said. "I'm hoping we can get the legislature to move on it, or the governor, or both."

"Isn't it more a federal issue?"

"We can't wait for them." Connor's voice rose. "Sweka told me the Nations have been pleading since the nineties. Canada's got a commission. I've got no leads on Diyanni's case. Time's up. And now seems to be a good time to get the media interested."

"I agree with you, but, well, my experience is the Feds can be touchy."

"Yeah, too bad. This has been on Justice's radar for a long time. It's a local issue too. When I call around on my case, I get frustration from the interested people and dismissal from everyone who says they have plenty of crime to pursue."

Kelly had no answer to that.

"Could you make it tomorrow afternoon for a brainstorming meeting here at the precinct?" Connor asked.

"Sure.

KELLY ARRIVED LAST, and was surprised to see Deputy Springer. The three men sat at a large, scratched conference table stuffed into a too-small, windowless room.

"Thanks for coming to the organizing meeting for what I'm calling the Missing Women Task Force," Connor said. "Even though most of the missing women are Indigenous, I think it might be better to be more inclusive. What do you think, Daniel?"

"So long as we don't lose focus," Sweka said, "I don't care what we name it. It's time to take the issue seriously, and the Nation wants to be part of the discussion. I'm sure all the local Nations do."

Connor gave them copies of a report he'd gotten from the Canadian Commission on Missing Indigenous Women. When he handed Kelly her copy and smiled at her with his large smoky eyes and impossibly long eyelashes, her crush reignited.

"The Canadians do love their commissions," Springer said.

Connor looked at him, surprised. "What do you mean?"

"The sheriff had me go to a Canadian meeting on those floating feet after we got one," he said. "Lots of people, not much progress. Seemed like they all pretty much thought it was a waste of time."

"I have to say, most meetings I've been to are a waste of time," Kelly said. "If we're going to do this, let's make sure ours aren't."

Connor sat back in his chair and laughed.

Why is he laughing? Kelly was a little hurt.

Connor straightened and looked Kelly in the eye. "We are not getting together to network or impress each other. We'll compare notes and brainstorm, make suggestions, and divide the work. And the meetings won't last more than an hour. Agreed?"

"Totally," Kelly said, and Sweka nodded.

"We could video conference some meetings, but I'm a little old-fashioned. I think face to face meetings are more productive."

Kelly nodded. Easy to get distracted, do other work, when participating from your desk.

"So, first up are resources. Daniel, you said you had trouble getting access to databases."

"Justice is talking about training tribal nation police and providing workstations so we can have access to national crime data. It hasn't happened yet, and when they do, they'll probably start with the large nations. Not us. We don't have the expertise or equipment to make use of the databases."

"Let's put that on the to-do list," Connor said.

"I heard the Intertribal Court System is working on that," Sweka said, writing it in his notebook. "I'll find out."

Connor handed each of them a list of known missing women. "This includes local reports from Galmenberg and the Nininpak Nation. I'm hoping you can add any from the County's missing person's files."

Springer nodded.

"I'd like to see what the three of you have on Diyanni so far too," Kelly said. "Therese and I have talked with a few people too. It'd be good to compare."

"Be sure to share with the rest of us," Springer said. "All three of us are involved with that case."

Sweka smiled at her. "Any help will be appreciated. I'll contact the other Nations and the Bureau. I've seen a number of postings. Hopefully we can make a comprehensive list."

"Let's meet again in two weeks with our lists and as much information as we can get about them," Connor said, gathering his papers back into a folder. "Kelly, can you stay a minute?"

Connor shut the door after Springer and Sweka left. "I know, I know, I promised to call. The Vandaroot case was a big distraction, but I'm sorry. How about we set a time for that beer? Saturday night?"

Kelly considered pretending she had plans, but that wasn't her style. "I should see if Ruth needs me to be somewhere, but that should be fine."

"I've been wanting to check out the Wayfarer. Sixish?"

Kelly's breath caught, and she hesitated. The Wayfarer was on the waterfront, far away from the gritty downtown and the crowds around the college. Elegant. Expensive. A date place. "Sounds great. I'll text Ruth and let you know."

Connor opened the door for her, and their shoulders brushed as she left.

ELEVEN

ON SATURDAY NIGHT, Kelly stared at all the blues and blacks in her closet and wondered what to wear. Jeans? A skirt? She didn't own much that could be called pretty and she never tried for sexy. Just a lot of business suits and jacketed dresses for work, and the loose pants and T-shirts she wore around the house. She should have gone shopping but didn't want to put too much energy into this probably-not-a-date. She fingered a silky green shirt scattered with little white shamrocks that Ma had sent her for Christmas and she'd never worn, deciding with black pants it would be suitably neutral. She let her hair hang loose, pulled a few gray hairs intruding on her dark hair, and took her picture in the mirror. Pretty good. The mascara and the blouse highlighted her green eyes and fair skin. Black Irish, just like Da. She texted the picture to Ma, who immediately texted "Beautiful" with a heart and a smiley face.

Everything about meeting Connor Andino for a beer tonight made her uneasy. She wasn't sure if it was because he was a cop or because she was so out of practice, but something was different. Uncomfortable. Exciting. She didn't own heels or any dressy shoes she realized, so quickly painted her toenails and put on sandals. She grabbed her long black sweater and headed out.

Connor was standing outside when she walked up, smoke rising from his hand in the calm night. When he saw her, he crushed the cigarette onto the sidewalk then threw the butt into a nearby trash can. "You look nice."

"Thanks," Kelly said. "I didn't know you smoked."

"I'm trying to quit," he said and then grinned. "Says every smoker every day."

"I quit about ten years ago," she said. "There are lots of days I wish I hadn't."

"So, my smoking isn't a deal breaker?"

"Nope. I've often thought if I knew I only had six weeks to live I might take it up again."

Connor laughed. "*Carpe diem.*"

But seizing the day or any kind of spontaneity was not who Kelly was. She decided not to share that just yet.

The bar was dim and quiet, with soft piano music playing in the background. They sat along the window facing the bay. The sun was setting, the trees from the nearest island disappearing into a mist. A sliver of orange and yellow lined the horizon and the edges of low lying clouds. As they talked, the dark deepened and the moon brightened. Small waves dispersed the moon's reflection and the few large boats moored nearby bumped rhythmically against their docks.

"You hungry?" Connor asked. "I know we were just going to get a beer, but I haven't eaten. And besides, it's my turn."

Kelly ordered a salad. Connor ordered Galmenberg's version of surf and turf—salmon and ribeye. The thought of it made her suddenly hungry.

"Can you put some salmon on my salad?" Kelly asked the waiter.

"Of course," he said.

"I'm glad you added that," Connor said. "I was afraid you'd want some of mine."

Kelly felt tongue-tied, not wanting to talk about work, fearful of talking about Ruth, not knowing what else to say. "Now that you've survived a winter here, are you ready to go back to the sun?"

"No," Connor said. "It is a little gloomier than I anticipated, but still better."

"Your family's not hounding you like mine did for years?"

"No."

Kelly sensed he didn't like this subject, hoped he could come up with something better.

"What made you decide to become a lawyer?" he asked as he put his napkin on his lap.

Kelly paused. "I don't know how to answer without sounding ridiculous."

"Try me."

Kelly debated whether to repeat the answer she always used in interviews, or the mixed-up motivations she thought were closer to the truth. She liked Connor, decided on truth.

"When I went to Seattle U I really had no plan other than to get far away from home."

Connor nodded. "Seattle is a Jesuit school, right?"

"Yeah, but I'd pretty much lost my religion by the time I got there." Kelly paused. She didn't want to talk about religion. Growing up, everyone she knew was Catholic. Her grandma said only Catholics would go to heaven, so she should be sure to marry one. Another thing to force from her mind. "What I didn't lose—this is the embarrassing part—is my conviction that I should make the world better somehow. I had no idea how, so majored in social work and took political science and government classes. My senior year I had to decide what next. My da and my brother Doug, a lot of the guys I grew up with, were cops and they were always complaining about how lawyers messed up perfectly good cases. I guess a part of me thought I'd be the one to fix the system."

"That's not ridiculous."

"Thanks." Kelly smiled at him. "I soon figured out after working for the AG why so many supposedly good cases were never charged. I became a convert to the process. Can't talk about the law now with my da. Always ends up in a fight." She looked at Connor to check his reaction, let out her breath when he leaned forward. Maybe it was time to talk about Ruth? "My messianic complex probably also led me to adopt my daughter Ruth."

"How old is she?"

"Fourteen."

"Her dad still around?"

"Never was. I've never been married and Ruth was abandoned." Kelly weighed telling Connor the whole story, decided that was enough for tonight. "How about you? Why are you a cop?"

"I suppose my motivations were sort of the reverse of yours. My dad's a defense attorney. He'd justify himself by saying all defendants are entitled to a vigorous defense, but he'd only represent those who could afford his three hundred dollars an hour services. If I were more academically inclined maybe I would have become a prosecutor, but being a cop appealed to me more. I like being out on the street, interviewing people, getting to know the community. The office part is the worst. My dad and most of his lawyer friends spent their days in their offices doing research or writing or talking to each other. Sounds boring to me."

"Sounds about right," Kelly said.

A server slid the salad and salmon onto the table, filled their water glasses, and left as quietly as he came. The moon had set, and only the running lights of a boat on the bay broke up the blackness beyond the docks. A sense of well-being, of possibilities, filled Kelly.

They ate quietly for several minutes. Kelly tried to figure out better, lighter, topics.

"Do you have any kids or pets?" Kelly asked.

"No kids. I have a dog, Buddy. A mutt I run with every day. You?"

"A cat. My daughter wants a dog, but they're so much more work. If we got one, it would have to be a dog that doesn't shed. But not a puny dog."

"Buddy sheds. Maybe a Schnauzer?"

"Yeah. Or a Standard Poodle?"

They spent the rest of the meal discussing the relative merits of dog breeds and past pets. When the waiter started coming over with increasing frequency, they got the hint. Outside the wind had picked up, and clouds hiding the moon grayed the dark sky.

Connor took Kelly's hand. "This was fun. Shall we do it again sometime?"

"Sounds great," Kelly said and Connor kissed her cheek.

SHE WAS TOO wired to sleep, and Ruth wasn't home, so she streamed *Game of Thrones*, turning off all the lights, mesmerized by the flashing screen more than what they were saying. The machinations of other worlds comforted her somehow. The Lannisters are bad, the Starks are good, and the rest are pretty much weasels. Kelly liked order. Liked knowing who were the good guys and wished life were more like that. Some people had a beer or a glass of wine when they came home at night. Kelly binge-watched TV. But not lawyer shows. Never lawyer shows. The few times she had, she'd ended up yelling at the screen correcting their process, telling the obviously innocent suspects to shut up.

Kelly looked at the clock before turning out the light. It was a half hour past Ruth's curfew. Where was she? She listened intently to the quiet, the downstairs clock ticking, Babs lapping her water then tapping her way across the kitchen tile. *Time to trim those nails,* Kelly thought sleepily. She heard a key in the back door and the soft whine of an unoiled hinge. Babs meowed, and Ruth shushed her.

Kelly decided to pretend she was asleep and didn't notice Ruth's late arrival. Not everything needs to be a confrontation, she reminded herself. Ruth was home. That's what mattered.

TRAVELER RAN FROM the lights that confused night with day, from the noise that never seemed to stop, where machines constantly screamed. No one here threw him a scrap or petted his fur, instead they waved their sticks and shoved him with boots. A truck with barking sounds followed him just before dark until he found a way through the trees where it could not go. Here, on the edge of the lights he found a hard path that led to another dark road. The longer he ran, the quieter the world became and when he heard no more human sounds, he stopped.

The dark was soundless and huge, the moon and stars hidden, the wind driving him forward. Too late, a whiff and noise of a machine, then two bright lights rushed toward him. He stood, frozen in their beams.

HENRY

2012

MILITARY POLICE GREETED Henry when the transport plane landed at Fort Lewis. Henry marched straight-backed with the officers to the Transition Center for out-processing. Henry handed his discharge papers to a young, uniformed woman whose smile turned cold as she read the papers.

"Sit over there," she said, pointing to straight-backed wooden chairs that looked as if they came from an old schoolhouse. Five other men sat there, backs against the wall and staring at the floor, hands between their knees. "It might be awhile."

And then he waited. None of the men wanted to talk, which was fine with Henry. Each time someone called a name and escorted one of the men behind a windowless steel door, Henry got up and paced. He walked past the woman at the reception desk five times before she told him there were vending machines in the alcove behind her. He used up ten minutes buying, then drinking, a soda and eating a bag of chips. As he waited, the MPs escorted in a woman and two more men in khakis all of whom sat in their uncomfortable chairs not saying a word to anyone.

Finally, a tall plain woman whose hair was gathered into a tight bun that pulled at her eyes and made her ears more pronounced called Henry's name. She took him into an alcove where she weighed him, took his temperature and blood pressure, and asked questions Henry was sure she already knew the answers to, such as his birthday and his type of discharge. She ushered him into a nearly bare examination room, told him to strip for the doctor, handed him a flimsy robe, and said he should sit on the paper-covered table to wait for the doctor. He held in his irritation. *This will be over soon.*

A doctor Henry figured couldn't be much older than him gave him a perfunctory physical exam, asked if he was clean, and prescribed him a low dosage of oxycodone for his pain.

"You know it's easy to get hooked on these," the doctor said, "so don't double up or use them with any other pain medication."

Henry promised he wouldn't.

Another silent nurse seated him in a new room with a scuffed table and four chairs. Brochures and single sheets of paper filled the clear plastic bins lining the walls. Henry was just about to pick one to read when a round man lumbered in. Henry wondered how long it had been since this guy'd been in uniform. He opened the file he was carrying, grabbed some brochures from around the room, placed them on the table, then dropped into the chair across from Henry.

"Good afternoon, Henry," the man said. "My name is Paul and I'm a counselor here. Do you have a job lined up?"

"No," Henry said.

Paul gave Henry a list of addresses and phone numbers. "Here's information about applying for unemployment and some places that can help you look." Paul gave him a brochure from the Veteran's Administration. "You can get most of the information about the VA online, but here's the basics about offices in Tacoma and Seattle. Do you have any questions?"

Henry shook his head.

"Do you have a place to live?"

"No."

Paul handed Henry a glossy advertising pamphlet that said "Rentals" in large letters. It showed a tall building with a pool and tennis courts that Henry was sure he couldn't afford and was probably filled with carefree twenty-somethings who would avoid him.

"Here's some listings to start. There are also motels and rooming houses that can work for temporary housing." Paul reviewed the file again. "I see you had some substance abuse issues and went through detox in Afghanistan?"

Henry nodded.

"I could get you a referral to outpatient counseling, Maybe even in person treatment, if you feel you need it."

"No, I'm good," Henry said. He couldn't think of anything worse than sitting around with a bunch of weepy addicts and sympathetic-but-tough psychologists. *Talk is cheap, and would make me angry*. He would have done it to stay in the Army, but not now.

"If you change your mind, contact the VA. And here's a list of Narcotics Anonymous meetings in the greater Seattle area. I strongly advise you attend them, at least until you're settled in."

"Thank you," Henry said, knowing he'd never go. He wondered how much longer, how many more of these ridiculous meetings he had to get through before he could leave.

"I just have a few more questions," Paul said. "How are you sleeping?"

"OK."

"Eight hours?"

"Six." That was an exaggeration, but Henry knew if he said less than six he'd be in this room forever.

"Any nightmares?"

Henry was sure this was a trick question. If he said no, Paul had to know he was lying. He'd been living in a war zone, for Christ's sake. "Once in a while. A couple of guys I knew died from IEDs and I see it again sometimes."

Paul nodded. "Understandable. Anything more?"

"No, not that I recall."

"Do you startle at loud noises?"

"No more than I did before I shipped out."

Paul looked at Henry intensely as if trying to decide if that was the truth. Satisfied, he asked, "Anything concern you?"

"I talked a lot of this through during my rehab in Afghanistan," Henry lied. He'd thought about his service a lot during the many hours alone on base. He didn't trust the doctor there, and he didn't trust these guys either. He just wanted to go.

"OK, this last paper has my contact information and some hotlines if you decide you need help or information." Paul stood and held out his hand.

Henry stood and shook his hand. Military police suddenly appeared to walk Henry to the guard gate. Henry saw a bus stop nearby and asked a guard where it went and where he could find a place to stay.

"Take the bus to downtown Tacoma," one said, a look of pity in his eyes. "Near the train station is your best bet."

"Thanks," Henry said, and sat in the bus shelter to wait again. Where next? he wondered. Not the farm or anywhere in rural Washington, of that he was certain.

THE BUS TO Tacoma dropped Henry in a sketchy neighborhood. He scoured a bulletin board in the terminal for room rentals, pulling little paper tabs for a few that looked promising. In his duffel he carried two pair civilian pants, four T-shirts, one white and one plaid dress shirt, a pair of brown oxfords, thirty Oxycodone, and a wallet carrying two hundred dollars, a debit card, his driver's license, and his VA card. That, the fatigues he wore, and the wages he'd banked were all he had in the world. He hoped it would be enough.

Henry wandered the nearby mall where nearly everyone thanked him for his service. He changed into his civilian clothes in the mall's bathroom and threw his fatigues into the garbage. Bought a pay-as-you-go cell phone and used it to locate the nearest room rental. He found it on a street lined with beat-up cars and cracked sidewalks, a faded brick two-story with only a sidewalk space between the buildings next to it. His new room was spare and dark, the only window looking onto the stained brick of the building next door. He opened the window and closed the blind in the hopes of letting out the room's stale smell. That night, the noise of cars and shouts and the occasional pop of what might have been a gun seemed almost serene.

The other men in the rooming house kept to themselves, locked the doors to their rooms, mumbled hello on the stairs but never looked Henry in the eye. Henry kept his eyes down too, not wanting to tell, or have anyone ask about, his story. He walked the neighborhood, wary of everyone he passed, as he searched for coffee and a quick meal. Every day he read the classifieds at a local diner then walked or took the bus to any employer looking. The newspapers said the economy was recovering from the Great Recession, but you couldn't tell that from the defeated faces of the men and women slumping on little plastic chairs in the employment offices Henry haunted. Most Human Resource Officers looked pleased when they saw he was in the military, but their smiles drooped when they saw he'd received a General Discharge and their eyes glazed when he explained his separation was for drug use.

"Could you pass our mandatory drug screening?" many asked.

"If you're OK with prescribed pain meds," Henry said, and that was the end of it.

He considered calling Grandma Janie, but he'd cut ties with everyone when he'd left three years ago. Never wrote, never told anyone where he'd gone. She was Dad's mom and would probably tell him, and Henry didn't want that. He used the local library's computer to look up Gloria, found out she'd married last summer. Grandma Janie was no longer at her old address, and he couldn't figure out where she might have gone.

As he lay in bed at night staring at the peeling wallpaper along the ceiling, hopelessness overwhelmed him. He had nowhere to go. No one to help him. A sleepless lethargy buzzed in his brain like flies near a closed window. He played his life in his head, trying to figure out where everything had gone wrong.

I did what I had to do. Every time.

And yet here he was. Maybe his life had been determined the day he was born, fated to be the child abandoned by his mother, abused by his father, ignored by everyone else.

I worked hard. I did my best. Didn't complain. Did everything the Army asked.

Henry felt a rage building. Rage at all he'd done for his country and how they tossed him aside because he needed to dull the pain to meet its demands. He remembered his dad's rages and for the first time wondered if it was life's unfairness that made his dad who he was.

Will I turn into him?

Henry's anger became panic. He took an extra pill to deaden the pain. His nightmares came in red and black, fog made out of sand, boys bursting into flame, screaming without sound. He woke filled with fear and an undefined longing that exploded into anger as the room came into focus.

Finally, after weeks of looking, a delivery service offered him part time work as a package handler on the night shift. The warehouse was cavernous and gray, its cement floors filled with snaking lines of metal rollers. Nearly empty now, the day supervisor told him the big trucks arrived at night from the airport and Portland, and his job would be to take boxes from the semis and send them along conveyor belts to sorters in the middle of the warehouse. Henry gaped at the maze of steel rollers leading from the truck bays to a tall line of shelving. On the other side were bays for the smaller trucks he would load for local delivery and one large bay for the trailer headed back to the airport.

Henry was young and strong and kept to himself when he worked, becoming part of the machine that emptied and loaded the trucks. His boss marveled and his coworkers resented how he could move more packages faster than anyone else, but Henry was never distracted by and didn't trust everyone's camaraderie. Behind his back they called him Mr. Roboto. After six months the company asked him to deliver packages, a lonely job where speed and silence was a boon. Henry felt himself losing control of his anger and was glad for the relative isolation of his delivery route. When he told the VA doctor the oxy didn't last twelve hours like it was supposed to, the doctor increased his dosage. He decided to take the pills every eight hours during his workday to calm himself down and allow him to work hard, but his nights were excruciating and relief came only in a bottle or from furtive purchases in alleys nearby.

Henry slept little. His life became ten-hour delivery days and weekends he worked overtime or drove a taxi, his car often carrying amorous couples or partying girls in tight dresses. He was invisible to them all. He spent other evenings alone at a casino or local bar. Sometimes a woman caught his eye and occasionally she invited him home. If one started looking for him too many nights in a row, he'd find a new bar. When he heard of an opening for a route to the small towns along the coast, he applied, favoring the longer drives and fewer stops. He found the hours on the road soothing, better than the horns and traffic and porch pirates in Seattle. He particularly liked Galmenberg with its wide bay and small town feel despite its size. It was a little too close to Dad's farm for his comfort, but not the nearest town. Maybe he'd move here someday.

AT A LOCAL bar one night a guy struck up a conversation with Henry, seemingly undeterred by Henry's silences or one word replies. Invited him to a party. Why not? Henry thought. No women worth having here tonight.

The party house wasn't far, and when they arrived, noise and light and laughter and music bombarded Henry. His new friend disappeared into the crowd and Henry made his way toward a patio where the noise and smoke were less oppressive. Outside two women smoked, their faces near and their cigarettes held above their heads. They stopped talking when Henry approached.

"Don't mind me," he said. "Just needed some air."

One of the women wore a tight-fitting black dress and looked at him as if affronted, but the other, a ginger with freckles on her shoulders gave him a bold smile before they went inside.

In the shadows, Henry watched through the open door. The women who looked good to him didn't stay standing alone for long and most of them seemed too crass, too obvious for him. Gloria would never go to a party like this, he knew. Gloria would never take you home for the night, either, he thought and turned his attention to those he thought might. Before he had time to decide, the redhead came back out.

"Do you have a light?" she asked, holding out a cigarette.

"I don't smoke," he said.

"What do you do?" she asked, leaning toward him.

"Most anything but that," he said.

"Want to walk me home? This party is too loud and you're the most interesting person here."

Henry wondered how she could know that but was happy for the invitation. As they left, he waved goodbye to his new friend from the bar.

HENRY WOKE WITH a start, disoriented, wary, all his nerves pulsing. Where was he? The window was in the wrong place. The bed softer. As the unfamiliar room took shape in the dim light seeping through the window shades, his panic grew. The soft snort next to him made him remember. The girl from the party. What was her name? A smell of stale smoke permeated the room. Henry had to leave. Now. Before she woke up.

On the way to the bathroom, Henry retrieved his clothes, his phone, his shoes. He dressed quickly, quietly. Four o'clock his phone said. He was sure she'd be mad when she found him gone, but his need to leave became urgent, insistent. She'd probably make him breakfast, but he didn't care, didn't want the obligation that came with it. Didn't want to know if she wanted to see him again. The door closed with a loud click. He ran the five blocks to his room through empty streets underneath the buzzing of yellow streetlights and their gaunt shadows. He stood under the shower until the water ran cold but his heart continued to race.

The room was dank, his sheets clammy as he tried to sleep despite the throbbing of his ankles and lower back. Instead, his mind sped between worry about complaints at work, anger at the Army, and irritation that he couldn't go back to last night's bar. He pushed away all thoughts of his dad, his mom, Gloria. When he sat up for a coughing fit that made his nose run and his eyes tear, he knew it was time for another pill. Then sleep.

2013

HENRY FOUND THE mornings at the warehouse excruciating. He had little tolerance for the inane instructions and comments at the morning meeting, and there was always something wrong with or delay in loading his truck. Control, control, control, became his mantra, but sometimes he lost it, like at yesterday's loader who had mis-tagged some boxes or the scheduler who gave him a delivery miles out of his way. And when he raised these issues at the morning meeting, they all looked at him like he was making idiotic points. His supervisor pulled him aside after one of his outbursts, telling him to be nicer to everyone.

The long trips up the coast gave him a lot of time to think about how his life turned out. He blamed his dad most of all, but he frequently fumed at the Army and the impossible expectations of his bosses too. He needed a way out but couldn't figure out how. His salary barely paid the bills. He'd moved into an apartment which meant he needed transportation so bought a used motorcycle. *Was I supposed to live in a rooming house the rest of my life?* Rent, gas, insurance, meds, everything cost money. *I can't work anymore than I already do.*

He loved his motorcycle, loved the feel of the wind as he drove, almost like parachuting from a plane. He knew he could lose his job if he lost his license, but sometimes he'd speed down rural roads or go a little faster than he should on the freeways to again feel that exhilaration and joy. He often stopped at a little turnoff along the coast to breathe in the salt air and watch fish leap. It was best at night when the moon reflected off the waves as they crested and crashed along the water's edge. Life could seem good then.

One weekend Henry was stopped for driving a little too fast, and he failed the field sobriety test. The officer, a fellow vet, gave him a ticket for speeding and told him to stay sober. Henry wondered if he should report it to the office at work, but decided it was so minor he'd just pay the fine and be done with it.

A few weeks later, the HR director asked to see him before the morning meeting. Presented Henry with a report showing his moving violation.

"When you became a driver for us," the director said, "you agreed to report all moving violations and gave us permission to see your driving record."

"I was on my own time," Henry said.

"Doesn't matter." The director slid a sheet of paper with Henry's signature across the table.

Henry glanced at the paper. "I'm super careful when I do my deliveries."

The director nodded sadly. "The company needs honesty from its workers, and this shows you were trying to hide your moving violation. So that's two strikes."

"I thought I only had to report the tickets I got on the job." Henry resisted the impulse to stare belligerently, slumping in his chair instead.

"And we've been getting reports of your lashing out at your coworkers for minor things. We strive for a harmonious atmosphere here where everyone helps and respects each other, something you seem unable to do."

Henry was outraged. Control, control, control. "When?"

"Your supervisor reported several instances of your shouting at the loaders and making snide and unhelpful comments at the morning meeting. He said he verbally counseled you about this on at least two occasions."

Henry sat speechless, his mouth open.

"For these reasons, we are terminating your employment, effective immediately." The director slid an envelope across the table and nodded to a security guard standing just outside. "Here's a check for two weeks' pay. Someone else is taking your delivery run today."

The guard walked Henry to his motorcycle. Stunned, Henry drove along the coast for hours, stopping only for gas and when he realized he was hungry. He didn't know what to do, how he could live. When he returned to his apartment, he checked his bank accounts and wondered where he could find a job, who would hire someone discharged from the Army and fired from his only other job.

I need to get away. Henry packed his duffel and realized he had little more than when he came back from Afghanistan. Just a motorcycle, his new gun, and a greatly reduced bank account. He tied his bag to the back of his bike and took off, he wasn't sure where.

VANCOUVER WAS LIVELY with tourists and others celebrating the end of winter. Henry grabbed a seat in the bar near a window to watch the sun drop on English Bay. Silhouettes of little dogs and their owners paraded along the beach in front of the orange-lined sky. He did love the Northwest, the water, the islands, the mountains, the ocean. And at least in Vancouver it was unlikely he'd see his dad. I should have come here instead of joining the army, he thought as he signaled for another beer.

Baxter, Talsen, Adanz, Wal, and all the other lost soldiers filled his head more and more lately. In his dreams they were joking. Moving. Alive. But the dreams always ended the same. Mutilated bodies on a stretcher. Kids exploding leaving nothing but a pair of flip-flops. Flames. Waves of dust.

It should have been me.

Peace came in a pill, if at all. The doctor prescribed oxy for him now, but the pain and the horror lurked at the edges of his consciousness always.

A group of guys at the bar grew louder and louder. On the television behind their heads the news flashed pictures of a bomb blast in a city Henry recognized as Kabul. He asked the bartender to turn up the volume, and one of the drunk men objected.

"A towel head blew himself up and took a couple of other towel heads with him. Who cares?"

Henry punched him in the face. Before he could pull out his gun, hands grabbed him from all sides and held his arms, his legs, and threw him to the ground. He smelled blood, felt its warmth running along his ears. Heard alarms in his head. A kick in his stomach, then another. The chaos above him came in waves as other arms pulled off his attackers. Blood and bile nearly drowned him. Sirens. Hands rolled him to his side, and he coughed blood. Pain. Dark.

HENRY LIMPED INTO the increasing wind sweeping from the bay, the morphine from his three days in the hospital wearing off. He barely saw the massive stone lions standing guard at the entrance to the bridge, but he sensed their unflinching presence. Lions Gate, he scoffed, because there are so many lions in Vancouver. On vacation one summer his mother had lifted him up to the smaller lions in Stanley Park, let him touch their noses and manes, saving him when he became afraid of how high he was and of the sound of the water rushing nearby.

Well, she's long gone, and there's no one to save me now.

Henry pulled off his sweatshirt and dropped it at the base of the bridge, hoping one of the city's wandering homeless would find it before the maintenance crew. His tactical vest would be enough. Wind whistled around the cables and towers and savaged his face once he reached the span over the water. He stopped at the observation area to watch the lighthouse below flash red. The container ships, their lights blinking, waited their turn on the other side of the peninsula, the dinner cruises had long since moored, and he saw no other boats lighting the dark water. He jogged toward the center of the bridge, pain nearly taking him down but reminding him of the truth of his life. The occasional squeak from his trainers on the cement was barely audible over the wind howling through the girders and the waves crashing into the pylons. He stopped where the lights lining the steel cables dipped the lowest to watch them spark on the black waves below. The far ends of the bridge reflected the yellow and red and orange of the city, but here, midstream, the bridge was dark and the few cars that flashed past the walkway seemed in another world. A world different from Henry's. One filled with places to go and things to do. No other pedestrians were foolish enough to brave the dark and wind tonight, and Henry stayed in the shadows, not wanting to attract the attention of any Good Samaritan or the occasional police car.

No one would hire him now he'd been charged with an assault and weapons violation. The court's leniency in setting bail was a small gift, but he had no intention of serving time. The world didn't need another man like his father, and Henry feared the heritage of his blood ran too strong. He felt its surging desire with every heartbeat. He grasped the railing, the cold biting his hands, and stared into the blackness below.

No one would miss him. No one would look for him. The tide and rough water would swallow him, and the morning fog would hide him. It was right and just that he should die. Henry pushed himself away, head tucked, knees bent and together, facing the wind.

TRAVELER LOVED THE humans who'd eased his pain. The sharp pain from the truck that knocked him down and the constant pain of hunger. They petted him after a man bound his leg, chased him in their wild games with balls and ropes, fed him, scratched behind his ears, called him Hal. He loved the warm house and table scraps. He even loved the dry kibble always in the white bowl just inside the barn. But he loved to dig and run too, especially at night when the cold called to him, when instinct told him to keep moving, warm his blood. At night, his humans didn't pay attention to what he did, and he could dig his hole under the fence and run through the forest and along the river.

A nearly full moon dodged the lumps of cloud, and bats circled overhead as Traveler loosened the dirt underneath the part of the fence his humans had not yet fortified. A distant owl oooohed. Soon the hole was large enough, and Traveler sped around the harvested fields, chasing a raccoon then a hare before heading toward the forest. He felt changes in the air and smelled snow coming, but not yet. He ran recklessly, changing direction when the smell of cougar intensified. Grizzlies kept their distance and deer ran from him, smelling the coyote and wolf in his blood.

Traveler ran toward the smell of water. He stopped at the sound of a motor and crouched at the dark edge of the forest as lights flashed over his head and glinted off the river before going out. This was new. No human had intruded on his night runs before. The shifting moonlight gave him glimpses of a shadow who stumbled in the dark, opened the back of a truck, and pulled out something long and stiff. The shadow stopped often along the rocks to the river, dropping his bundle then dragging it again. He rolled it into the river, then used a branch to push it into the fastest part of the river. It moved like a log down the stream, catching on rocks then lurching forward. Traveler stayed crouched until the motor grumbled, lights flashed on, and moved away.

Traveler padded toward the river. Familiar scents hung over the water. Behind the trees on the opposite bank, he saw yellow eyes stare and then leave. He drank as the sky lightened and birds began their morning songs. Snow flurries lifted and dropped in the wind and hoarfrost hung from branches. He ran toward home, over yarrow and wild hyacinth, past the waking beavers, and otters. A few shards of sleet hung from his coat when he reached the pasture. He was hungry.

TWELVE

CURIOSITY PIERCED CONNOR'S Monday morning lethargy when Springer handed him the DNA report from the floating foot case. The bones in the shoe belonged to an army paratrooper named Henry Penthell, discharged three years ago.

"The sheriff said to give this to you," Springer said. "Said it's kind of a reverse missing person's case since I couldn't find any report of him missing."

Connor looked up and nodded. The Army rep he called asked for information but wouldn't give any, told him to send proof of identity and death and she'd get back to him.

"Can you at least give me his birthday?"

No.

"His next of kin so we can do a notification?"

No.

Frustrated, Connor did a birth certificate search in Washington, and was pleasantly surprised when he located a Henry Penthell, DOB June 27, 1991, parents Samuel and Debra Penthell. A quick search led him to a record for Samuel, who lived in a rural area south of the Hotsaem River.

"Go," the sheriff said. "If you can get a DNA sample, we can verify. Better than waiting for the Army."

Connor followed a maze of country roads toward the Penthell farm, passing large squares of pasture interrupted by stands of large pines. He wished he lived out here, close to the river where he could fish or just sit and watch the water rush over the rocks. Most people want to live near the ocean, but Connor preferred the contained river, fields, and forest over the wild unpredictability of the Pacific. No floating feet here. Peaceful.

When his GPS said he'd arrived, he turned on a rutted drive leading to a small house surrounded by bare dirt. A loose screen door squeaked on its hinges in the breeze and scraped the rotting boards of the front porch. Layers of paint, blue and white, peeled away from gray fascia boards. Behind the house stood a large barn, its faded red scraped gray along the doors and where large enclosures were attached. In one pen three large and four smaller pigs snorted as they dozed in the sun.

Connor knocked several times, but when no one came he tried the barn.

"What do you want?" a voice said. Deep in the gloom a man sat smoking a cigar.

"I'd like to talk with you about your son," Connor said.

"I've no son."

Damn, Connor thought. A dead end. "Do you know a Henry Penthell?"

"Henry left years ago. Joined the Army someone told me. He never told me. You here to say he died in the war? Fine. Go now."

"He didn't die in the war," Connor said. "We think he committed suicide. We need to verify his identity and notify his next of kin."

The man stood and walked into the dim light coming through a window high up the barn's wall, hands in the pockets of his dirty overalls. He was wiry, tough-looking, years of labor showing on his stringy age-spotted arms and rough hands. "You think?"

"We found a shoe with his foot in it. At Galmenberg Bay."

The man laughed. "Henry, one of those floating feet. Fitting."

His reaction disturbed Connor. He understood they were estranged. Had to be since there wasn't any report of Henry missing. But funny?

"We were hoping you could help us figure out whether it was suicide or something else."

"Nope."

"When did you last talk to him?"

"Five or six years or so? Like I said, he didn't even tell me he joined the army. Just left one day."

"Why'd he leave?"

"Who knows with teenagers. One day he walks out the door and I never see or hear from him again." The man kicked a stone toward the sleeping pigs. "He'd just graduated high school. I thought he'd finally be decent help around here."

"And you don't know why."

"His momma died when he was young. I probably wasn't much of a dad, but farming ain't easy. I thought he was OK, then one day he got all fierce and quiet. Did his chores, went to school, but never talked. Drank my whiskey when I wasn't around, and I beat him good for that. He didn't seem to care."

"If you could give me a DNA sample we can know for sure if it's your son."

"Why you telling me he's dead if you don't know it's him?"

"Army records say the DNA is of a Henry Penthell. Maybe it's a different Henry."

"Don't know many Penthells, and none of my relatives have the name of Henry. That was Debby's family." The man laid his cigar in a scuffed metal can. "Doesn't matter to me who this foot belongs to."

Connor had met a lot of crusty old men both here and in Nevada, but this guy made him uneasy. His greasy hair curling in strands underneath his Seahawks cap, dirty clothes, and body odor made Connor think he hadn't washed in a long time. The way he didn't care about his son. "We'd still like a sample of your DNA so we can close the case and deliver his remains to you."

"Nope."

"Why not?"

The man leaned toward him, fisting his hands. "You want my DNA, you get a warrant. I have a right to privacy. Don't nobody take that away from me. Especially not the fucking government. And you can keep the body. Or foot." He laughed. "My Henry died a long time ago."

Connor backed up and put his hands in front of him. "OK. Would you sign a release to give us access to Henry's Army records?"

"Get out," the man said, his voice low and threatening.

THIRTEEN

KELLY'S PHONE BLARED at three a.m. Fear jolted her awake.

Ruth.

The phone's display said, "unknown caller."

If this is spam, they will get a piece of my mind.

"Kelly Flynn?" a vaguely familiar man's voice said.

"It is. Who's this?"

"Greg Springer. I'm calling from the sheriff's office in Galmenberg. We picked up your daughter Ruth. Can you come pick her up?"

"What happened? Is she hurt?"

"She's not hurt. It's better if you come by."

Kelly quickly brushed her teeth, threw on a sweatshirt and jeans, and rushed into the garage.

The streetlights made starbursts like Van Gogh's paintings in the light fog. A few squad cars roamed the otherwise empty streets. As she approached the downtown, a few men shuffled past the darkened storefronts or sat on the stairs of the courthouse, its well-lit towers a beacon. More activity surrounded the sheriff's office—a young man in handcuffs being pulled out of a car, two officers on a cigarette break, red and blue lights flashing atop an SUV.

Inside, a breathless Kelly asked about Ruth, and the desk sergeant directed her past the orange plastic chairs and scuffed linoleum toward a room in the back. Ruth was slouching next to a uniformed woman who stood when Kelly entered. Kelly pulled a chair next to Ruth.

"What happened?"

"I was just hanging out at Pioneer Park when these Nazis arrested me," Ruth said, looking at the floor.

"You must know that calling them 'Nazis' won't help you."

Ruth shrugged and crossed her arms.

"Hi, Kelly." Deputy Springer came into the room. He sat on a chair behind a narrow table and motioned Kelly to come nearer.

"She says she was in Pioneer Park when you picked her up?"

"Yes," Springer said. "She and two young men were smoking marijuana in the park. None of them were old enough, and they were in a public place, so that's two possible offenses. Ruth told us she doesn't know where it came from, that the boys were already smoking when she joined them. Has she used marijuana before?"

"I don't believe so." *And how would I know?* All the parenting articles said she should check Ruth's room, smell her clothes, check her laptop. Kelly had given up on all these things, preferring peace to the inevitable fights. *I'm a bad mother.*

"That's good. She says this was her first time. We've warned her about its effects on a developing brain." Springer handed Kelly a pamphlet and another piece of paper. Kelly recognized them. They handed out the same things at her office. "Here's some information the Cannabis Board put out. Please read it and talk about it with Ruth."

"I will," Kelly said in her humblest voice. "What time did you find them?"

"Half past midnight. So, it's a curfew violation too."

Kelly nodded. *Should I tell him I think that law is unconstitutional? No, I should not.*

"We're not citing her this time, but we can't let it go if it happens again."

"I know. Thank you."

Deputy Springer rose, shook her hand, then walked her and Ruth to the lobby. Ruth scowled.

A heavy silence surrounded Kelly and Ruth on the walk to the car and during the drive home, Kelly's anger building as she tried and failed to come up with a way to address this. When they parked in the garage Ruth said, "I'm sleeping in tomorrow."

That was too much. "Oh, no you're not. You were supposed to be home by eleven. I shouldn't need to wait up to make sure you are. I should be able to trust you. And you know you're too young to smoke dope. And you do it in public for the world to see. What were you thinking? Do you even think?" Kelly stopped herself before she became even more aggravated.

"What the big deal? OK, I'm not twenty-one. That's just arbitrary."

"Do I really need to explain to you that your brain keeps developing until age twenty-five and drugs can affect that development?"

Ruth glared at Kelly.

"I'll get you the research if you don't believe me."

Ruth's mouth formed a thin line.

"Choices have consequences. The first consequence is you are grounded for two weeks, and your curfew is ten for the month after that."

"That's so unfair!"

"No, it isn't. C'mon. I know they've gone over all this at your school. Don't act so outraged. You made a choice, now live with it. How you could have thought smoking weed in a County Park was a good idea is beyond me."

Ruth punched her fist to open the door. "OK Karen," she said, heading toward her room.

You little shit is what she wanted to say but grimaced to hold back the words she feared would drive Ruth away forever. The years of holding her tongue clawed at her throat, made her head buzz. Yes, she would make demands. She was tired of being silent. Silent to avoid confrontation with Ruth, with coworkers, with her father, her teachers. Silent when the boys at school assumed a girl couldn't play ball, couldn't be included, when even school counselors directed her toward elementary school teaching when she expressed interest in the law. Years of losing jobs to less qualified men and having to prove herself by working harder and longer than any man in her office. Years of sexual innuendo and disdain disguised as humor. Years of holding in her anger and hurt and fear that she was the fraud many men thought she was. And now dismissed as not worthy of an explanation by her own daughter? She wanted to explode, howl, rip her clothes into tatters.

"We will talk about this," Kelly shouted, unable to stop herself. "I told the officer you hadn't smoked before. Have you?"

Ruth clenched her hands.

"Who were those boys?"

Ruth's eyes narrowed into angry slits.

"Why didn't you come home on time?"

"You treat me like a child," Ruth shouted.

"You. Are. A. Child," Kelly said. "Legally, and you've just proven it. You act irresponsibly and when caught refuse to admit you were wrong. You lay the blame for anything bad that happens on other people. You expect other people to fix your messes. If you don't want to be treated like a child, then stop acting like one."

Kelly feared she'd gone too far. But it was true. How could Ruth ever learn how to be a functioning adult if she never accepted responsibility for her actions?

"Me!" Ruth said in a high pitched scream. "Me? Look at yourself! You're such a damn rule follower you take no chances, don't even try to see that some rules are wrong. You just shuffle along like some automaton, doing the 'right thing,' never examining what you decided to believe years ago. 'Look how noble I am adopting some drug addict's baby.' You think that gives you a pass on being a caring human being. I refuse to be like you."

Kelly ground her teeth. Ruth certainly knew which buttons to push. Tears burned in her eyes. Some of what Ruth said was true, some of it she had thought about herself. How would they survive this? She thought about Diyanni and a sudden rush of fear infused her anger.

"Don't be stupid, Ruth. The world is dangerous. Adolescent boys are dangerous. Drugs are dangerous. Girls on empty streets in empty parks in the middle of the night are prey. How can you not know that?"

"Your mind's been poisoned by your job. I can tell if somebody's shady. You think serial killers lurk in every alley."

"And where do you think they lurk?" Kelly knew she was shrieking, knew that didn't help, couldn't seem to stop. Her job did make her wary, suspicious. But the things she'd seen, the cases she worked on frightened her to her core.

"I think I'm more likely to be shot by some loser at school than kidnapped in the middle of a city park smoking with some boys I know." Ruth picked up Babs, who had been circling their feet and clawing the carpet.

Kelly froze. How hard it must be to go to school every day wondering if some sad kid with a gun picked today for payback. There was no way to protect Ruth from all the terror and evil thrust in front of them every day. Kelly wanted to, but couldn't.

She pulled Ruth toward her into a hug and cried, "Oh, sweetheart. I couldn't bear it if anything happened to you."

Ruth stood stiffly and shook Kelly off. "And you are always angry at something. Deadbeat dads, police shootings, judge nominations, court cases that don't go your way—"

"For good reason."

"The list goes on. And then you turn that anger at me. I walk on eggshells around here, wondering what will set you off next. Can't you be a mom who bakes cookies and welcomes my friends and thinks me incapable of doing anything wrong?"

Kelly paused, chastened. "I think you're capable of great things and I love you. That's something, isn't it?"

"I will never live up to your expectations, and I'm tired of trying. You have so many. Why can't you like me as I am?"

"I love you exactly as you are. Is it wrong to want to help you be the best you can?"

"You see? There it is. You're always watching, pushing, judging. So I hang out with a couple of stoners. They don't try to change me."

"So it's my fault you got caught smoking dope in a public park?"

Ruth huffed and turned to leave. Kelly sunk into the nearest chair and put her head in her hands.

"Would it help if we went to counseling together?" Kelly asked.

Ruth shrugged. "Probably not."

"Can we try?"

Ruth bolted toward her room.

FOURTEEN

SHERIFF NISSER HUSTLED past the deputies' cubicles, his thinning hair plastered to his head. Several people dodged into open spaces to let him pass. "Body found along the Upper Hotsaem near Kellashan and Hemlock Falls," he said when he reached Connor's office. "Check it out. Homicide's on another call and it might be one of your missing girls."

Galmenberg Bay's murky gray told the mood of the sky, so different from yesterday's calm bright blue or the wild whitecaps before last week's storm. Connor was ready for the sun and warmth to stay awhile. He drove past miles of bare farmland, sheep herds, and the occasional horse until the hills became steeper and pine trees blocked their view of the snow-covered mountains. The increasing dark and quiet away from the farms felt ominous. He pulled up next to the medical examiner's van, the only human activity he'd seen for miles.

A crime scene technician emerged from the woods and waved. The narrow rocky path through the pines toward the river made approach difficult. Dr. Green and the forensics team were already in the water. A fallen log and several boulders stopped the body from continuing downstream.

"Pretty remote," Connor said to the crime scene technician as he signed the log. "Who found her?"

The technician pointed to two girls on three-wheelers parked along the bank, holding the leash of a large feral-looking dog. The dog's tall ears twitched when anyone talked and he stared at Connor with golden eyes. "Looking for their dog. We've got their information, but I asked them to wait for you."

Connor pulled on his waders and sloshed toward the body, making slow progress as the cold water with small ice floes crashed against his legs. The woman seemed young, with long black hair floating in the currents intertwined with twigs and leaves. That and her flimsy red dress made Connor think of Diyanni. Could it be? Her arm was wedged underneath a log, and the rest of her body lay in odd angles. She was not dressed for winter: no coat, no gloves, no shoes, not even panty hose. Bruises and slashes marred her face enough to make her unrecognizable but not as much as Connor would have expected from scavenging animals.

Connor crouched next to Dr. Green. "Fairly recent, I'd guess."

"And that's why I'm the medical examiner and you're not," Dr. Green said. "See this discoloration on her face and arm? Could be evidence of freezing. No telling when she died. At least not yet."

A shock wave ran through him, and he looked toward the mountain ridge. Snow stayed in the glaciers and above the tree line on the mountains, but so far in October there'd only been a couple of overnight freezes at this elevation. "Frozen higher up? You think she was dumped upriver?"

"Or stored in a freezer. I'll know more after the autopsy."

"Anything to identify her?"

"Not that we've found so far."

Damn. Connor pulled off his gloves and threw them in the collection box. Cold bit at his face, the trees funneling wind his way. Time to talk with the witnesses. As he approached, he saw they were young. They wriggled nervously on their three wheelers, stomping their feet and blowing warm breath into their hands. Both were dressed in navy parkas and snow pants, hoods drawn tightly with scarves loosened around their faces. They looked at Connor with a mixture of fear and excitement and jumped off their machines as he approached. The dog gave a quick warning bark.

"Didn't expect this, did you?" Connor said, hoping to calm them.

"No, sir," the taller one said, as the other patted the dog, told him it was all right.

"I'm Detective Andino. What are your names?"

"I'm Shelly, and this here's Jessy. And Hal."

Jessy gave a little wave, but kept looking at the ground.

Connor could sense their fear, so he bent down to let Hal sniff his hand. Hal did, but stayed alert and growled when he tried to pet him. "I don't think I've ever met a dog named Hal."

Shelly grinned. "Grandpa found him hurt on the side of the road. Grandma named him, said he looked like a Hal."

Jessy scratched Hal's ears.

Now they were smiling, taking turns petting Hal and telling him what a good boy he was. Connor hoped they were comfortable enough to talk. "Did you touch the lady in the river or move anything?"

"No, sir," both said.

"How about Hal?"

"No, sir," Jessy said. "He found us later."

"So, tell me what happened."

Shelly pulled her red plaid scarf away from her face, winding and unwinding it in her hands as she talked. "Hal dug under his fence and ran. He does that a lot. Dad says we need to tie him or lock him in the barn, but he comes back. By the time we got to our three wheelers to chase him he was already in the woods. We were just about to give up when I saw a bunch of birds circling and swooping and thought maybe Hal was checking out the same thing those birds were. That's when we saw her."

"We called our mom to tell her what we found, and she called you guys," Jessy said.

"You get cell service out here?" Connor asked. "Because I don't."

Jessy pulled an orange walkie-talkie out of her coat's pocket. "Mom makes us carry these when we're on our three-wheelers."

"Smart," Connor said. "Go on home. If we need something more we'll come by your house, okay?"

They both nodded but didn't move, mesmerized by the activity in the water. Green's staff worked a plastic tarp underneath the body and what looked like a large, torn canvas bag, a slow process. Once they'd lifted her out, log, bag, and all, they put everything else that had touched the body in evidence bags and bottled several water samples. Connor put on a new pair of gloves and waded back into the water, feeling around the riverbed, hoping to find a cell phone or anything that would help identify the woman. Whatever might have been there, was gone now.

KELLY SMILED WHEN she saw Connor's name on her caller-id. It had been weeks since she'd heard from him, more since their dinner and what she now was sure was not a date.

"Do you have a way to get a hold of Therese?" Connor said when Kelly answered. "I tried the number I have, but it didn't go through."

"She lives on the Rez, and cell service is pretty spotty. I can drive out there if it's important. Why?"

"We found a body."

Kelly's stomach clenched, fear overtaking her hopefulness. "Do you think it's Diyanni?"

"Age seems about right. Red dress. Face is pretty messed up so it's hard for me to say whether it's her from her picture. I can send pictures, but I think that might not be so helpful either. Upsetting. We want to know if Therese will try to identify the body. Or we can wait for DNA results."

"I'm sure she'll want to come."

"If you tell me how to get to her place, I can go."

Kelly hesitated, decided she should be there. "Let me drive. It's hard to describe the turnoffs, and I've been there before."

"OK," Connor said. "And I'll try Officer Sweka again."

THE BAY'S WILD waves seemed unruly, menacing, as Kelly drove past. The spray drenched several people standing on the rocks along the shoreline, almost knocking them into the ocean.

"Idiots," Connor said.

As they approached Therese's house, Kelly saw her sitting on a bench with Officer Sweka. Both looked grim.

Sweka walked toward them as they left the car. "I told her you found a body," he said in a quiet voice.

Connor sat on the bench next to Therese. "I brought a couple pictures, or we can just head back to the coroner's."

Therese looked straight ahead and refused to look at the pictures.

Sweka took them from Connor's hands and examined each. "Hard to say."

"I need to see her," Therese said.

"Would you like to come with me or Daniel?" Kelly said.

Therese hesitated, looked at Sweka.

"Why don't you ride with Kelly," Daniel said. "I'll go pick up Layla, meet you there, and we can drive back together."

Therese nodded. On the way to the coroner's office, Therese sat in the back and stared out the window. She said nothing as they drove, parked, and climbed the steps into the county building. She said nothing when Daniel and Layla arrived. Dr. Green led them into a warmly lit room with couches, chairs, and a small wooden table with four chairs and a carafe.

"We have some pictures we'd like to show you," Dr. Green said.

"I want to see her," Therese whispered.

"And if you think it's her, you may. But let's avoid that if we can."

Therese looked unconvinced. Kelly, too, had expected to be led to a cold, sterile room to look at the body, but this did seem more humane.

"Just try," Kelly said.

The first two pictures were the ones Connor had shown Kelly, a picture of a dark-haired woman laying on a metal table, a sheet covering all but her face, then a close-up of her face marred by discoloration and several gashes.

"I don't know," Therese said.

Dr. Green then turned over another picture, this one showing a faint diagonal scar along the right abdomen. "Has she ever had surgery?"

"Yes, her appendix," Therese said, tensing and looking at Layla with a wild expression.

The third picture was of an oval, kidney-shaped birthmark, dark brown and covered with hair, on the woman's chest several inches below her shoulder. At the sight of it Therese began wailing. She stood, walked to the door, came back, collapsed onto a soft chair in a corner of the room. A woman Kelly had barely noticed approached Therese and crouched in front of but did not touch her. Layla sat on the arm of the chair and put her head on Therese's.

"Your daughter has a similar birthmark?" the woman asked.

"Yes," Therese said, burying her face in her hands.

No one spoke or moved. Kelly didn't know what to say that could be any comfort. Everything that came to mind seemed trite. Unhelpful. Maybe even offensive.

"I'm so sorry, Therese," Kelly finally said and others echoed.

Therese stood and wiped her eyes. "I want to see her."

"Are you sure?" Dr. Green said. "We have enough for a preliminary identification. We're doing a mitochondrial DNA test that will verify whether she's your daughter."

"I want to see her."

Dr. Green led them to a dim room with stainless steel lockers lining the walls. A single gurney covered by a sheet sat in the middle of the room.

Connor handed her gloves. "Are you ready?"

Therese nodded, and Dr. Green pulled the sheet to the body's chest.

Tears slid down Therese's face. She brushed strands of hair from the body's face, touched the birthmark, held her hand. She stood quaking silently for several minutes.

"Oh, my girl," she said and turned away.

Kelly wanted to hug Therese. Should she? Was that appropriate? Kelly wasn't a hugger, couldn't figure out why she wanted to now except she had no words. She put her hand on Therese's shoulder. "If there's anything I can do . . ."

Therese leaned into the crook of Kelly's arms, foundering. Kelly held her tightly, letting go only when Therese pulled away.

"When can I bury her?" Therese asked.

"We still have tests to run to help us catch whoever did this," Dr. Green said. "We'll call you as soon as we can."

"The Nation will take care of everything," Daniel said. "Exactly how you want it."

Layla took Therese's arm as they left. Daniel walked ahead and held his cell phone to his ear.

Following behind, Kelly wondered about the funeral. She wanted to pay her respects. She'd never been to a Nininpak funeral, didn't know if it was private. Whether she'd be welcomed or an intruder. *Should I send flowers? Make her a casserole?* That's what she'd do for Clara or Dave. *Will Therese be alone? Should I offer to stay with her? Have her stay with me?* She tried to think what she'd want if Ruth died. Nothing, that's what she would want. No, that's not right, she'd want to scream as loud as she wanted and be as rude as she wanted and have somebody bring food and make her eat it but she probably wouldn't.

Oh, Therese. Nothing will fix this. Nothing will help.

When they got to the parking lot, Kelly decided to say what she felt was right. "Therese, I mean it, anything I can do to make things easier."

Therese looked at Kelly with her red, puffy eyes. "My families will come and I'll stay with Layla. But come to the memorial if you can."

"Of course, I will," Kelly said. "Just let me know."

EXHAUSTED, KELLY LAY down when she got home, waking when she heard Ruth slam the kitchen door. Babs lay next to her, raised her head when Kelly sat, then nestled back into the tunnel of sunlight that came from a gap in the curtains to pool on the quilt. Kelly quickly straightened her blouse and hair and met Ruth at the top of the stairs.

"You're home early," Ruth said.

"Went with Therese to identify Diyanni's body today."

"Sorry, Mom."

Kelly started to cry. "I need you to be safe, Ruth. I need us to be okay. Please don't shut me out. Please come to me if you need help."

They sat on the stairs, Ruth looking stunned as Kelly cried.

"Mom, I'm careful. Really. I am. And we're fine. I just need you to chill, to trust me."

"I do. Mostly. But I don't want to miss any signs you're in trouble or in over your head." Kelly could feel Ruth bristle. *Oh, no, I've said the wrong thing. Again.* She pulled at a loose thread in the carpet. "I want to be supportive. Not be that mom who gets interviewed on TV who says, 'I had no idea she was being bullied' or ready to commit suicide, or shooting heroin, or building a bomb." Ruth let out an exasperated sigh. "I want to know who you are and what's troubling you, to be there for you when you need me to be. I didn't really have that when I was your age. Just a lot of rules about what good girls did and didn't do."

Ruth shrugged. "Feels like that to me too. Except I'm not sure what the rules are. You want so much from me. It's exhausting and you get all disappointed when I screw up and there are some things I just don't want to talk about."

Kelly knew Ruth had a point. She was overprotective. Couldn't help herself. Ruth was too important. "Maybe a counselor could help? No, don't roll your eyes at me. Somebody who can be more objective and helpful because they're not in the middle of it. We don't have to go together; you could have your own. I'd feel a whole lot better knowing you were talking to somebody even if it isn't me."

"OK, Mom. I'll give it a try." Ruth stood up, went to her room, and closed her door.

"I'll make an appointment," Kelly shouted and hoped she heard a muffled okay.

FIFTEEN

THE MEDICAL EXAMINER'S autopsy report sickened Kelly. Diyanni's body had been frozen, partially thawed, then refrozen. Bones had been fractured post-mortem in places consistent with the body having been kept in a small space. Like a freezer. *Who does such things?* The thought made Kelly shiver. She dreaded telling Therese, hoped Connor or Daniel would do it. Maybe Therese didn't need to know that little piece of horror until they caught the guy. A blood test revealed Diyanni'd been drugged. And she'd been pregnant. A boy. Kelly was amazed some DNA under Diyanni's fingernails survived submersion in the river, amazed at all the things the forensic scientists could figure out.

I should get Ruthy that dog she wants, she decided suddenly. It would make her happy, maybe even keep her safe when she's home alone or walking the neighborhood.

<Still want a dog?> Kelly texted.

The answer came immediately. <YES>

<You'll have to walk it. And pick up after it>

<OK>

<Check out the adoptable dogs website. We can visit the shelter this weekend>

<YAY>

AS THEY APPROACHED the shelter's front door on Saturday, Kelly heard the yips and barks of the dogs inside. The smell of urine and bleach grew stronger as they neared the heavy steel doors where they kept the animals. Kelly had brought stray dogs here, and they were always wary and skittish. Ruth stopped to say hello to each one she passed in their narrow concrete stalls, a wire gate on one side, a doggy door to the yard on the other. The noise became almost unbearable as each dog begged for attention.

Kelly wanted to rescue a dog but feared their pasts would make them difficult or dangerous. *Maybe we should get a puppy from a ranch breeder. They're not all puppy mills.*

As they neared the end of the first aisle, they saw Eddie. The sign on the gate said he was probably an Airedale/Standard Poodle mix around five years old. He stood tall, his head tilted, curly ears twitching and tail wagging as he watched them. Kelly liked that he wasn't barking or pacing, just looking at her as if she were as interesting to him as he was to her. Ruth held her hand out to let him sniff. He licked it then gave a single bark.

"Hey, Big Eddie," Kelly said. "What's a great guy like you doing in a place like this."

Eddie bent his front legs then stood several times as if to say, "Play with me."

"That's a cool dog," a young man in a heavy apron and knee-high boots over his jeans said. "You want to see him in the yard?"

"What do you think, Ruth?" Kelly asked.

"For sure," Ruth said.

The young man directed them to a fenced grassy area with several picnic tables. Most of the other dogs came into their small enclosed outdoor areas to watch and bark. The young man leashed Eddie and led him out his back gate to the noisy disapproval of the rest of the pack. Eddie bounded toward them but stopped a few feet in front of Ruth and crouched.

"I think he likes you," Kelly said.

Ruth took the leash and walked with him. She saw a frisbee along the fence about the same time Eddie did. He took it in his mouth then dropped it at her feet.

"May I take him off the leash and throw it?" she asked the young man.

"Leave his leash on, but you can let him run."

Eddie circled the fence line, barked a quick hello to his caged buddies, ran to the frisbee, picked it up with his teeth and dropped it again. Ruth threw it toward Kelly in the far corner, and Eddie caught it midair, ran back to Ruth, and waved his head until she took it.

"Can I play, too?" Kelly asked Eddie, and for the next few minutes they played keep away with Eddie usually winning.

Eddie seemed disappointed when they stopped throwing until Ruth scratched his ears. He lay down, seeming to beg for a tummy rub. Ruth complied.

"So, what do you think?" the young man asked.

"He's great. I'm just not sure we're home enough for him. And we have a cat."

"He gets along with the cats here," the young man said. "Don't know about your cat."

"Babs gets along with the neighborhood dogs okay," Ruth said, a pleading whine in her voice. "She just ignores them. Please? Can we try?"

Kelly knew the dog would be more work than the cat was, and likely more affectionate. Maybe that's what Ruth needed, some unconditional love and acceptance. Some responsibility, too.

"OK," Kelly said. "But if they can't get along, we'll need to bring him back."

"They'll be fine," Ruth said. "Babs can be your pet, and Eddie will be mine."

The young man broke into a big smile and led them to the office. After a half hour they left with Eddie, a thin leash, and a small bag of food.

On the way home, Ruth sat in the back seat of their Outback with Eddie, who seemed content to be petted as he stuck his nose out the side window. Kelly watched them in the rearview mirror, seeing Ruth smile more than she had in a very long time. Eddie bounded out of the car into the garage and raced inside as soon as Kelly opened the house door. Kelly grabbed the cat dish from the floor and put it on the counter. Undeterred, Eddie put his paws on the countertop and stood, sniffing.

"Not for you," Kelly said. She looked at Ruth. "Looks like he needs some training."

"Down, Eddie," Ruth said, pulling at his collar. "Let's go outside."

Ruth and Eddie went out the back door, and Kelly watched them run in circles in the fenced yard. Within seconds Babs came in through the kitty door and meowed.

"A bit much, little girl?" Kelly asked Babs, lifting her to the counter. This was probably where Babs food would be from now on.

KELLY SAT AT the kitchen table drinking coffee and going through her pile of mail. Babs slept in a square of sunlight coming through the back door despite Eddie's excited barks and scratches wanting to come in. Kelly supposed she should get a bigger pet door, but guessed that Babs appreciated the ability to get away from Eddie sometimes. At least she'd stopped hissing at him and swatting his nose. Eddie thought that was an invitation to play and Babs only escape was through the kitty flap that barely fit Eddie's nose.

Kelly tore open a letter from the Casino, fearing it was some timeshare offer until she saw Layla Mos was the sender. It was a formal invitation to Diyanni's public memorial service, to be held at the Casino Ballroom this coming Saturday. She hadn't heard from Therese or Daniel during the two weeks since Therese identified the body, didn't know if she should call or leave her alone. She was glad to be invited.

Diyanni's death shook Kelly. They didn't know yet what had happened, but whatever it was had been awful. *Young girls are so fragile. So hopeful. So naive, so stupid sometimes.* Tears dripped onto the invitation, warping its paper. She knew she'd done many stupid things too, could have ended up in a river too. And Ruth. *How can I protect her?* one voice inside her head said. *You can't, not completely,* another voice said. *You are not in control.* She sobbed. Babs the cat wound around her ankles and meowed. Eddie's scratching became more frantic and she opened the door to let him in when she got up to find a box of tissues.

Kelly was still crying when Ruth burst in the front door, calling for Eddie. He bounded to greet her. Ruth's voice had a happy lilt as she told him what a good boy he was and did he want his ears scratched? Of course he did.

Ruth came into the kitchen after a few minutes of happy yips, saw Kelly crying, and asked, fear in her voice, "What happened?"

Kelly pushed the invitation across the table, still unable to speak. Ruth read it. "This is for that girl you were looking for? The one they found in the river?"

Kelly nodded and looked up to see tears in Ruth's eyes. She took Ruth's hand.

"Would you come with me?" Kelly asked when she finally found her voice.

Ruth's hand tensed, and fear flashed in her eyes.

"Okay," Ruth said.

SIXTEEN

WHEN A FULL DNA search failed to find a match, and the FBI declined to run a partial match search, Connor requested a local search of partial DNA for the trace found on Diyanni's body. Two days later he gaped at the new report. His face burned, a sliver of fear and excitement ran up his spine, and the sounds in the room deadened. A familial, likely paternal, match to Henry Penthell.

His mind flew to Sam. He was a nasty old man. Was he a murderer too? Could he have been the guy in the casino video? Or was it some other close relative? There were lots of mean-looking, gun-toting recluses living in the backwoods. He prayed a quick thank you to God and to Henry for giving them a lead. He wished he'd gotten Sam's DNA. Well, they could get a warrant now.

Maybe. What if Henry was adopted? No, the birth certificate took care of that.

Sheriff Nisser rose so quickly from his desk to grab the report his coffee sloshed onto the carpet and a picture of one of his dogs dropped to the floor. He plunked back into his chair, eyes wild then focused. "I'll call state patrol. You call the FBI. Have the lab run tests for partial DNA for other unsolved cases."

Connor called Kelly.

"Are you positive? Go-ahead-call-the-mom positive?"

"Don't call Therese yet. I'll call Officer Sweka. We don't have a suspect, just that he's related to that foot on the beach. I would like to see those Casino videos again though. I've met Henry's dad."

"Maybe State will be interested in our task force now," Kelly said.

"We can hope."

Sheriff Nisser called a meeting. "FBI says it won't run national partial match search, although they'll run a full match search on the DNA found on Diyanni Hupt."

"We've already done that. FBI's sticking to their privacy policy?"

"Apparently so. They're willing to run the lab work once we have a suspect."

Connor's skin prickled with anger. The whole point was to find a suspect. Well, at least they could look for more partial matches in the state database.

BY THE NEXT morning, Connor and the sheriff were on their way to Olympia. The State lab had found an identical match to the trace DNA on the body of a young woman found three months ago along the Columbia River. Patrol had asked all local jurisdictions to rerun DNA found on bodies in similar cold cases.

"What do they mean by similar?" Connor asked as they drove.

"We'll cast a wide net," Nisser said. "Any unsolved rape case or involving a dead woman. I pity Seattle PD; they've got a lot more than we have. They'll probably start with young women found near a river."

"That seems random. How about the ones where the convicted killer says they're innocent?"

"Let their lawyers ask for that. You know they will once this gets out."

Officer Sweka was already in the boardroom when the sheriff and Connor arrived. He held several files. They nodded to each other and sat together near the front. The room buzzed with private conversations and greetings as police officers filled paper cups from a coffee urn on a table in the back. Even detectives wore their dress uniforms. A scan of the crowd showed Connor that most present were from state patrol and the Seattle Police Department.

The Assistant Chief for Investigative Services led the meeting. "I assume you've read the memos and emails that have been flying past us the last twenty-four hours and brought information about what might be the most relevant cases we should focus on."

After an hour of discussing missing women, bodies, unsolved rapes, and the ethics of familial DNA searches, a clearly frustrated Seattle detective said, "Don't you think we're overreacting?"

"I think it's about time we dug a little deeper into what happened to these women," Sweka said, his voice shaking with anger. "And I knew the young woman in this case. I want to find her killer. So, no, I don't think anyone is overreacting. I think we're finally coordinating."

The murmur in the corner where the downstate people sat together hinted they disagreed, but several tribal officers nodded and crossed their arms. Connor realized his arms were crossed too.

"In any case, no one has the resources to investigate every missing or unidentified woman, every body, with the intensity that Cascadia County has given this case," the assistant chief said, smiling at Sheriff Nisser. "I admire your persistence and think it's about time we follow up on Nininpak's and Cascadia's request to form a task force. Let me know if you're interested in working on it, and in the meantime forward your relevant cases to my office. Thank you all."

"A task force won't find our killer," Sheriff Nisser mumbled.

"Maybe not," Connor said. "But we have another partial match to Henry Penthell. That should get us a warrant for his dad's DNA."

"I think we should try for a warrant for the whole farm," Sweka said. "If he's involved, you can bet he'll do a big cleanup."

"It's worth a try," Sheriff Nisser said. "Call that deputy county attorney you've been working with. What's her name?

"Flynn," Connor said. "She was involved with the shoe too."

"I'LL SERVE THE warrant," Sheriff Nisser said.

"He'll definitely resist." Connor was glad to have the sheriff's company on this trip to Sam Penthell's farm. The warrant covered only collection of a DNA sample from Sam, the judge saying she'd issue the full warrant only if it matched. The lab obtained a fast test that would tell them in a few hours whether Sam's DNA matched what they'd found on Diyanni. They'd stay on the property until they had results. FBI was on standby, waiting until they got the DNA results. Then, Connor knew, they'd want to take over the investigation.

The long roads and empty fields leading to the Penthell farm seemed ominous this time. Eerily quiet. Only an occasional cow foraging in the distance. Connor's dread grew the closer they came. *No safety anywhere. But at least in the city there are witnesses.*

The quiet and Connor's body armor squeezed as they approached Sam's house. Connor wondered where were the pigs and cows, the skinny dog, he'd seen last time. A few raptors circled high in the sky.

"He was in the barn last time," Connor said as he got out of the car.

Sheriff Nisser opened the rear door and retrieved his hat from the back seat. "We need to try the house first."

A shotgun blast rang out and blew out the passenger window on the sheriff's car. They dropped to the ground and scrambled for cover.

"I warned you," Sam shouted from somewhere. "Get back in your car and leave."

"We have a warrant, Mr. Penthell," Sheriff Nisser said.

Connor wondered how the sheriff could be so calm. His chest hurt and his hands shook as he radioed for help. "Shots fired!" he shouted to whoever answered, and as if to corroborate, Sam fired again, this time taking out the front fender.

"Find cover and wait for backup!" Sheriff Nisser shouted. He opened the nearest car door for a shield.

All was quiet for an agonizing minute. Then Connor saw smoke coming from the barn.

"Fire!"

Sheriff Nisser swore. Connor called for Fire Response.

Now the flames were visible through the open barn door.

"Where's Penthell?" Sheriff Nisser shouted. "Andino, can you see the back of the barn?"

Connor ran along the side of the house toward the back to get a better view. Another shotgun blast. Well, at least they knew where he was.

They'd have no trouble getting a second warrant now.

Connor heard a helicopter overhead and sirens approaching. Soon the field surrounding the house was swarming with cars and vans labeled SWAT and FBI and Galmenberg.

"Come out with your hands up!" an FBI agent yelled over a loudspeaker.

Sam came out, holding his shotgun above his head. Immediately seven agents crouched into firing positions.

"Lay down your weapon!"

Sam sneered at the man holding the megaphone, his stance and face oozing with hatred. "Ruby Ridge!" he shouted, shaking his gun before dropping it. It fired when it hit the ground, taking out a piece of the house roof. All the officers rushed him, slamming him into the ground.

Connor thought he heard Sam laughing over the cacophony of sirens and helicopters.

Half the barn collapsed before the fire trucks arrived, and the dry hay made it unlikely they'd be able to save the rest.

Deputy Springer arrived just as the agents were dragging a handcuffed Sam to the FBI van. "Jesus," he said to Connor. "I thought you were just serving a warrant."

Connor picked up the red cap that had fallen off Sam's head during the scuffle. He looked toward the burning barn, considered throwing it into the flames.

"That's evidence," Sheriff Nisser said, handing him a bag.

Agents with yellow crime scene tape were busy cordoning off the farm as fire trucks arrived. Connor felt overwhelmed and directionless, deaf to the sirens and rushing water and collapsing structures.

"We've got the warrant to search the premises," FBI Agent-in-charge Leo shouted.

Forensic techs filed out of three vans. One group headed toward the house, one toward the fenced pens, and the third skirted the barn and went toward the outbuildings and sheds.

"Any idea what we should be looking for?" Agent Leo asked Sheriff Nisser.

"A freezer? Our medical examiner said the body we found could have been in a freezer for a while."

Connor pulled out a picture of Diyanni from his clipboard and pointed to her necklace. "Her mom said she liked to wear this necklace and she couldn't find it in her apartment after Diyanni went missing. It wasn't on the body when we recovered it."

Agent Leo nodded and brought the picture to the forensics investigator giving out assignments. The scene was chaotic, people shouting, phones ringing, all over the whoosh of fire and water and the cracks from falling timbers.

"My guys saw a freezer in the back of the house," Leo shouted.

Connor and Sheriff Nisser put booties over their shoes, changed their heavy gloves for nitrile, and went in.

The house smelled of bacon and mildew and years of dust. Pulled shades covered all the windows. Crusted dishes sat in the sink and an overflowing garbage bin filled a corner of the kitchen. They flipped the light switches, and it remained dim as most of the bulbs were missing or burned out.

Connor tripped over something on the floor and shined his flashlight over curling linoleum and the leg of a broken chair. Little black flecks covered the kitchen area, and a mouse carcass lay in the corner. He wrinkled his nose. In the living room overstretched carpeting covered in muddy footprints lay beneath a worn couch, two chairs, and several cans and bottles of beer. On the wall hung a large, flat screen TV. He pushed open the drapes to a view of Agent Leo directing his team to the smoldering barn.

Sheriff Nisser slowly turned the knob then pushed open the door to the first room along a hall that led toward the back of the house. He waved Connor to the next door. That room held a single bed with a bare mattress and a desk. On the desk were several old textbooks and a curling diploma for Henry Penthell. In the closet were a pair of snowshoes and a pile of jeans, T-shirts, and underwear. Dust covered every surface.

"Clear," Sheriff Nisser shouted out the front door to summon the crime scene techs.

The freezer was on a screened porch in the back. One tech collected samples from inside, while another took pictures of the piles of clothing, towels, and ashtrays on the floor.

"Looks like there's blood pretty much everywhere in here," a tech said from the kitchen. "Or bleach."

"Not sure this guy knows what cleaning supplies are," Connor said.

"Let's check out the barn," Nisser said. "The fire's out."

The ground was bare and hard-packed on the few hundred feet to the barn. Agent Leo was inside, staring at a heavy chain from a still intact truss beam.

"What's that for?" Connor asked.

"City boy," the Sheriff said. "That is where you hang an animal after you've killed him. To drain the blood before butchering. No point wasting luminol underneath there. Of course there's blood."

"Hopefully some to collect and test," Agent Leo said. "The fire ran over most of the floor."

Bile rose in Connor's throat as he realized what Agent Leo meant, and he put his hand on the nearest post to steady himself. Through the damaged walls he saw several pigs chewing grass in a back pasture next to a long metal building and a travel trailer. Processing this scene would take weeks, longer if they started finding anything tied to the missing women.

"Let the forensics teams do their jobs," Sheriff Nisser said. "It's time to talk to Mr. Penthell."

SEVENTEEN

AS HE WAITED in the squad car, Sam screamed expletives and pounded the windows with his handcuffed wrists. On the way to the precinct, he turned backward, his mouth moving wide and eyes angry at Connor and Sheriff Nisser in the following car. A helicopter overhead drowned out all other sound. A swarm of police cars and news vans surrounded the County garage when they drove in. Reporters were everywhere. Law enforcement officers and FBI agents provided a gauntlet as one pulled Sam out of the car and shoved him forward. Sam shouted his innocence and his hatred for the government. The officers kept blank expressions, their stance aggressive as they provided a path for the deputies dragging Sam inside and keeping the shouting newscasters and cameras out.

Agent Leo, Sheriff Nisser, and Connor followed the custody officers into a back interrogation room, skipping the front desk. Sam continued to thrash and swear, so the deputies handcuffed him to a table and left him alone in the room. The observation room filled quickly. Sam yelled for water, and Agent Leo went into the room with a bottle.

"Give it to me, free my hands," Sam yelled.

"Mr. Penthell," Agent Leo said in a calm voice. "I can't undo your hands until you calm down, but I'm happy to squirt some into your mouth if you're thirsty."

"Torture, huh? You're going to waterboard me, aren't you? I'm thirsty. Denying me water is cruel and unusual punishment."

"Would you prefer I put it in a bowl?"

"That's right, treat me like an animal. I haven't done anything, but deny me my rights."

"You shot at a detective and the sheriff," Leo said.

"They came onto my private property," Sam raged. "I warned that detective to stay away."

"They had a valid warrant."

"No they did not. I'm a sovereign citizen. They had no right."

Connor sighed as he watched. There was no arguing with these so-called Constitutional Patriots. Why was Leo even bothering? Book the guy and let him cool off in a jail cell.

But Agent Leo kept on in his calm, droning voice, telling Sam he was being charged with threatening a police officer and resisting arrest, that he had a right to remain silent and to an attorney, and offered water. Sam continued to rant. After a half hour, Leo asked a tech to swab Sam's cheek for DNA. Sam kicked and screamed and thrashed, but a large sheriff's deputy held Sam's head as the lab tech quickly performed her task.

When they finished, Agent Leo leaned across the table. "Those charges I told you about? Those are state charges and now the sheriff's guys will book you, but don't you worry, little man, we'll get you for killing that Nininpak woman too. And any other federal crime we can prove."

Sam froze and watched silently as Agent Leo left, a stunned look on his face. He remained silent when Deputy Springer and another officer entered, informed him of the charges, read him his constitutional rights, forced his hands open for fingerprinting. Then he spit at them. "You got no proof cause I ain't killed nobody. I don't know what you think you know, but I ain't talking to you or nobody."

"Should we try to interview him now?" Connor asked Sheriff Nisser.

"Nah, no point. Let him talk to an attorney, see if that will calm him down."

REPORTERS SWARMED THE courthouse for the arraignment and bail hearing and kept calling calling calling anyone they could think of, any name associated with the case. They called every member of the sheriff's department, every county prosecutor. Each night on the news, beautiful women and men told the world in their concerned voices about the latest observation, clue, and hypothesis, with pictures of the melee of Sam's arrest behind their heads or on inset pictures on the screen. They called Sam the Mt. Baker Butcher.

Ruth was sitting on the couch and staring at her phone, mouth open, when Kelly arrived home. "Is this the guy who took the woman we searched for?" she asked, never taking her eyes from the spectacle playing out on her small screen.

Kelly turned on the television. "They think it might be, but they don't have any evidence yet. The guy that was shot at? He's a friend of mine."

Ruth looked up, and Kelly thought she saw a glimmer of interest. Maybe even respect. "Wow. Too close."

Kelly sat next to Ruth and put her arm around her shoulders. "Way too close. Does it explain my anxiety a little?"

"I guess so, but it's still irritating," Ruth said, leaning her head back onto Kelly's arm. "So what really happened?"

"All I know is what I've heard on the news. I knew they were going out there because I worked on the warrant, but I had no idea this would happen. My boss stepped in when they called about the shooting."

Ruth turned toward Kelly, excitement in her eyes. "Why do they think it might be him?"

Kelly wanted to keep Ruth's interest, to seem like a hero in her eyes. But she knew she couldn't tell anyone, not even her family, the details of what she did. "I'm sorry, honey, I can't talk about that."

Ruth's eyes dimmed, and she crossed her arms. "As usual."

They watched the broadcast silently.

Ruth got up when the station began the weather report. "What's for dinner?"

"How about I heat up that leftover stew?"

Ruth shrugged and nodded. "I'll stick it in the microwave if you want to keep watching."

Kelly smiled. "Thanks."

AFTER THREE DAYS at the scene, the forensic and clean up teams had found many strange things, but it was unclear what, if any, were related to missing women. They found blood almost everywhere, but most were mixed samples and much of it tested as animal blood. The insides of the freezer on the porch and the two that survived the barn fire looked more promising but provided mostly dusty overlays of fingerprints and mixed blood samples. The mixed and degraded samples made identification difficult and inconclusive. They found an old skull buried in the piggery but had no identification yet.

How long has he been at this? Connor wondered.

Sheriff Nisser thought they had enough to prosecute Sam for Diyanni's murder with what they had, but Paltik wasn't so sure.

At the police agencies' meetings to review the forensic reports, a ghoulish humor grew as they wondered what each new discovery might mean, what could be released to the press, what the press might do with it. Handcuffs, a bloody rake, hair ties, a lacy red bra, a curly gray toupee, a gold tooth.

"What's that?" Connor said, pointing to a picture of a string of beads behind the freezer partly covered by dirty towels. The next picture showed a scuffed carved orca attached to a string of red and black beads. He rifled through the boxes of evidence bags stacked on the floor and pulled out a bag containing a carved cedar necklace. Its strap was broken, and many of the beads were missing. The letters *C X* were visible on the back.

"It looks like Diyanni's," he said, brushing his eye. He held it up to Sheriff Nisser, who dug Diyanni's picture out of the file to compare. In it, a smiling Diyanni wore a vibrant version of the same necklace.

"Well, maybe he's not a Robert Pickton or Gary Ridgway," Sheriff Nisser said. "But we've got him for one murder anyway."

"YES, I'LL COME," Kelly said when Connor asked her to accompany him and Dan Sweka to tell Therese what they'd found at Sam Penthell's farm. "But please don't make me show her any pictures."

"No," Connor said. "Officer Sweka will do that."

Kelly had been mesmerized by the grainy photographs she'd seen, and every night she and Ruth watched the news hoping for explanations. In the office, in the stores, and on the local talk shows people talked of little else. And now this. Another connection to Diyanni.

Connor and Daniel waited for Kelly at the casino, and together they drove the short distance to Therese's home. They tramped over leaves and pine needles to the hush of the wind. Therese sat on a lawn chair underneath the awning and near a carved post Kelly didn't remember seeing the last time she'd been here, watching the river and petting the huge orange cat. Therese's face changed to fear, but she didn't get up, just petted the cat with more vigor until he'd had enough, jumped off her lap, and disappeared inside.

Daniel unfolded a chair propped against the side of the house, sat facing Therese, and took her hand. "We have a picture we'd like you to look at."

Therese nodded.

Connor motioned that Kelly should get closer, so she took a chair and sat next to Therese. Connor did too and handed Daniel a photograph of an orca necklace.

Tears gathered on the edges of Therese's eyes, but few fell. She nodded again. "That's like the one my mom gave her. Are her initials on the back?"

"There are initials on the back. I should have copied that picture because I can't remember what they were. We'll test it for DNA, and you can see it."

"Aren't some of Celia's pieces in the Seattle museum?" Kelly said. "We could get a museum official to testify to its authenticity too."

"Can I have it back?" Therese asked.

"Not until after the trial, I'm afraid," Connor said.

Therese's eyes pleaded with Kelly.

"Unless he confesses, right detective?" Kelly said.

"Yes, as soon as he's convicted, but so far he's proclaiming his innocence."

Therese sat back into her chair and closed her eyes, emanating resignation and despair. The awkwardness grew as her silence extended. Kelly thought Daniel would know better when they should leave, so she didn't move.

"We should eat," Therese said, rising.

Kelly's first impulse was to say no, and she could see Connor shake his head, but Daniel gave them a look that shut them up.

"We would be honored to eat with you," Daniel said.

They followed Therese inside where the wood stove had warmed the room and the cat lay sprawled on the couch and looked at them as if he had no intention of moving.

"May I help you with anything?" Kelly asked.

Therese gave her a wan smile and bowed her head a little. "No, thanks. It won't take long."

She put a pot of water on the stove, then pulled out cheese from the small refrigerator. She filled a plate with a mix of cookies and crackers and bread and offered some to each of them. She then put boiling water and loose tea into a teapot, and handed each of them a mug. They watched in silence as she filled their mugs. Finally she sat.

"Thank you," Kelly said, and the men echoed her.

Serving them seemed to have calmed Therese. "It's hard to know a terrible man hurt Dee, but still I'm glad you've told me. I hope your children outlive you."

An icy pain filled Kelly's chest. She couldn't imagine the pain of losing Ruth, so much worse than the pain of terminating her and Brad's child which she'd barely survived. What sorts of things went through Therese's mind when she tried to sleep at night?

"I am so sorry, Therese," Kelly said. She felt like she'd said the same thing a thousand time already, but had no other words. "Please let me know if there's anything I can do to help.

A flash of anger washed over Therese's face. "Find other mothers' children. Stop it from happening to anyone else."

"I wish I knew how to stop it," Daniel said. "But we'll do our best to find them."

Therese nodded and gathered the dishes. Daniel stood. Therese thanked each one of them as they left and accepted Kelly's quick hug. No one talked on the short drive back to the casino.

Alone in her car on the drive home, the world seemed oppressively heavy to Kelly.

EIGHTEEN

THE MEDIA ATTENTION intensified again once the FBI announced they had a match with Sam's DNA and traces found on two bodies. The FBI, Attorney General, Sheriff Nisser, and Prosecuting Attorney Paltik held daily media briefings until mid-November, but still reporters called. As the weeks passed, most reporters waited for press releases and sporadic press conferences, only a few hardy investigators driving out to the Penthell farm to photograph the teams of forensic scientists in their hooded white biohazard suits moonwalking behind the fences and yellow tape. Paltik intended to prosecute the local charges himself, but made Kelly the second chair and responsible for building the case. When reporters found out, they called Kelly at work, on her cell, rang her front door.

Kelly told Ruth not to answer the door, not to talk with the reporters. "They are not your friend, and no matter what they say they only want some break that will put them on national news."

"Don't you want people to know?" Ruth asked.

Don't I? Kelly wondered. "Not at the expense of Therese's pain. Let them do a story on the rest of the missing women and let the legal system do its job in prosecuting Sam."

Ruth looked thoughtful. "Why do you care? Seems like all publicity could help."

"I don't think so," Kelly said. "Sure it's good to sympathize with a grieving family when they've had a tragedy, but at some point it's too much. Especially for someone as private as Therese. And where were all these reporters when we were trying to get Diyanni's picture out? And I hate that Sam is getting all this attention. I've heard he's already started getting love letters. It's sick."

Ruth laughed and covered her face. "I'm sorry. It's not funny. But love letters? Really? Who would do that?"

"Every serial killer has a fan club. I don't get it. But the real tragedy is the more media attention Sam gets, the easier it is for his attorneys to claim he didn't get a fair trial. He's in custody. Let him rot there. Reporters should try to find the missing women."

"What happened to innocent until proven guilty?"

"There's proof enough for me. I wouldn't be prosecuting him if I didn't believe he was guilty."

"Fair enough," Ruth said, tilting her head as she watched Kelly. "I have seen some reporters talking about the missing women, with charts and percentages. That's good, right?"

"Yes," Kelly said, calming a little. "Knowing there's a problem is a start. I do hope the attention will get the State and the Feds to put more resources toward searching, and making local police more receptive when people come in to say someone's missing." She dropped onto the sofa, feeling overwhelmed. "I suppose it is hard to tell the difference between a runaway and someone who's truly missing, maybe hurt or dead."

Ruth sat next to Kelly. "You take this personally."

Tears rolled down Kelly's cheeks, she wasn't exactly sure why but they felt like angry tears. Ruth took her hand.

"Don't worry, Mom," Ruth said. "I'll be careful."

SEE ME THE note on Kelly's desk said when she arrived at the office the next morning. No name, but she knew it was from Paltik. She hoped it was good news or a new assignment but feared it might be something else.

"Close the door and have a seat," Paltik said.

Kelly relaxed when he didn't seem angry or upset. The last time she sat in his office was for her performance review. *Is it time for that again?* It couldn't have possibly been a year already.

"How are you handling this Sam Penthell case?" Paltik asked. "You seem different, troubled, less animated than usual."

Kelly didn't know how to answer. Her personal life was none of his business, but she hadn't thought it affected her job. And she thought she was handling finding Diyanni's body as well as anyone could expect given how terrible it was. She was glad they'd arrested Sam. Maybe there would be a kind of justice this time. For a change.

"How do you mean?" she said. "Is my performance less than you expect?"

"You're a fine attorney. I have no issue with your performance. But I sense something's wrong and because it's recent, I have to think it's related to this serial killer. So, I'm asking. If you'd like to see a counselor, go. I'm sure the County's insurance will cover it. you could even see the Sheriff's Department's counselor if that's easier."

Kelly was wary, and his concern seemed intrusive. Misplaced. He liked to see himself as a father figure, but he wasn't her father, and he should leave her alone if she was doing her job and doing it well. She clenched her hands and jaw as she searched for something to say.

"Now, don't get all tense and worried," he said. "I'm not suggesting anything like a mental health fitness exam, although if I were you, I'd choose someone other than the departmental counselor if you're worried about confidentiality."

Kelly felt tears burning her eyes. *Oh my god, I'm such a girl.* She fought them back.

"It's just a suggestion," he said. "And you don't need to tell me whether you do or not and I won't ask. But this job can be tough sometimes. We see a lot of terrible things and can start to believe the world is a cold and cruel place. A place not worth living in. If talking to someone might help keep that at bay, you should take advantage."

Kelly looked Paltik in the eye and saw concern, kindness. "I'll think about it."

"That's all I ask," he said.

Kelly walked back to her office, avoiding the furtive glances of the staff who wondered what just happened. She closed her door and typed randomly at her computer but she was thinking rather than working. Maybe she should have an individual counselor as well as going to family counseling with Ruth. She knew Ma had counseling sessions with the priest back home, and although Ma never shared what they talked about, the sessions had seemed to help her. Kelly had assumed Ma was unburdening about some minor sin her saint of a mother blew all out of proportion. Was it?

Kelly hadn't talked to a priest since her annual confessions during Lent at college. And she'd never confessed or even told anyone about her abortion.

Like those old men have any idea what it's like to be sixteen and pregnant. Who are they, who is anyone to condemn me?

But, still, it made her feel guilty to go to Confession and not even mention her biggest sin. So, she stopped going. She remembered being a little envious of her study group for a Theology class when they talked about the freedom the Sacrament of Reconciliation gave them. She never felt that, and she was sure telling some celibate man that she'd had an abortion would not make her feel free or reconciled or whatever they wanted to call it. It would just give them all one more reason to condemn her.

And what about Brad? Why is he off the hook?

One of her high school friends told her the scandalous news when Kelly was at Seattle U that Brad had gotten Mary Sue pregnant during his sophomore year at Purdue, married her, gave up his football scholarship, started driving a delivery truck. Ma told her a few years ago he was a lay minister in their parish and had three lovely children.

Yes, I'm still bitter.

She'd never told Ruth about the abortion, not sure she ever would. She feared it would be one more piece of painful ammunition Ruth could shoot at her during an argument. Yes, having separate counselors was a good idea.

"WE SHOULD GO to Chicago for Thanksgiving," Kelly said as they ate dinner the Thursday before.

The family counselor told them they needed to eat together at least three times a week and talk to each other, and they were trying. Sometimes, like tonight, it was takeout chicken and mashed potatoes that Kelly got from the drive-thru on her way home, but they'd agreed to talk and eat for at least a half hour. This was their third week and as usual they had run out of things to say. Or that they were willing to say. Planning a trip seemed a fairly neutral topic.

Ruth smiled and looked interested. "Sort of short notice, isn't it? The news is always talking about how crowded the airports are during Thanksgiving weekend."

"You're probably right, but if I can get tickets would you like to go? My case is at a holding pattern right now but will likely pick up in December so Thanksgiving is better than Christmas. Plus it's less likely to snow."

"I'd love to see everybody," Ruth said, grabbing another biscuit from the paper bag. "Can we go downtown?"

"I'll call Grandma after supper."

Kelly sat at her computer, checking flights and trying to decide if she should reserve a hotel. It's what she'd prefer but her mom would be offended. The flights were ridiculously expensive unless they flew on Thanksgiving Day. Ma always served the turkey at two. There was an overnight flight that left Seattle late Wednesday night and got into O'Hare at six Thanksgiving morning, but they'd have to come back either Saturday or Monday. Ruth chose Monday. Well, why not. They hadn't gone to Chicago in years.

Kelly's mom cried when she called to ask if they could come, wanted them to stay longer. Of course she and Da would pick them up, or maybe just Da because she had to get the turkey in the oven. Of course Kelly and Ruth must stay with them. Sure, they would go downtown on Friday, look at the Christmas decorations in the windows on State Street, eat at the Christkindl market, shop. Ma's excitement built as she listed all the things they could see, the people they could visit. And mass, of course, on Sunday.

Kelly stopped smiling as she remembered Brad went to her parent's church. Would she see him? The idea panicked her. Maybe Ruth would assert her atheism and refuse to go.

THE OVERNIGHT FLIGHT was brutal for Kelly, but Ruth slept most of the way. Kelly was too full of anticipation and dread to sleep, too tired to focus on reading, so she snacked on the candy and nuts they'd grabbed at the airport as she worked on the puzzles in the in-flight magazine. She texted when they landed. Da was already in the cell phone lot. The terminal was calmer and emptier than usual when they arrived, most of the stores and restaurants closed. They stood in line for Starbucks, knowing it would take more than a half hour to get to her mom's ever-brewing coffee pot. Da was talking to an officer who wanted him to move on when Kelly and Ruth reached the curb. Kelly apologized to the officer and wished him a Happy Thanksgiving as Da put their carry-ons into the trunk of his gold Cadillac whose wide grille bared its teeth at her.

"Nice car," Ruth said. She called shotgun, and Kelly was happy to relax in the back seat.

Da smiled and proudly told her all of its features. He'd always loved his cars, got a new one every three years. This one was brand new.

The house was quiet when they arrived. Ma hugged Kelly, then stood with her arms around Ruth for what seemed like several minutes but, Kelly admitted to herself, probably wasn't. The smell of butter and roasting meat filled the very warm kitchen.

"Ma, I didn't sleep on the plane. Would you mind if I lay down for a while?"

"Of course, lie down. How about you, sweetheart? Did you sleep?"

Ruth nodded. "I'm wide awake. Can I help you with something?

"Talk to me," Ma said, grinning. "And snap these beans. Kelly, I've got you in the room at the top of the stairs to the left."

Kelly took off her sweater and pants, then crawled under the sheets, blanket, and chenille bedspread of the double bed in the room. There was something comforting, familiar, and strange about the room, its cross on the wall, the furniture the same as was in her old bedroom. She quickly dozed, waking to the sound of car doors slamming. She wasn't ready yet. She'd pretend to sleep a while longer. A few minutes later Ruth knocked on the door and came in.

"Aunty Mary and her family are here. Grandma wanted me to tell you," Ruth said, sitting on the bed. "And it's my turn for a nap."

Kelly sat up. "Are we sharing this room?"

Ruth shrugged. "I don't know, but you've messed it up already."

Kelly got dressed, bracing herself for the mayhem to come. She and Ruth led a quiet life, and she knew this day would be anything but.

Mary, the only other sibling from out of town, drove from Milwaukee with her husband and two young boys. The boys had been in the car too long, and immediately went outside to throw a ball with their dad. Mary stood in the narrow kitchen with two pies, apple and pumpkin, that she put down to hug Kelly.

"Hey, stranger, how are things in the Great Northwest?" Mary said.

"Great," Kelly said. "What's up with you?"

Mary was five years younger than Kelly, not yet in high school when Kelly had left for college and never returned. They weren't close. Kelly wasn't close to any of her siblings, and what little connection they'd had growing up had long since withered. She wondered how her life would have been different if she'd stayed, or moved back. If Ruth's life would have been better with aunts and uncles and cousins and grandparents. What did it matter? Their life was what it was. She'd seen enough dysfunctional families in her job to know that being related by blood didn't necessarily make families happy.

As she and Mary expanded and set the table, more people arrived.

"Set up a kid's table in the living room where we can see them," Ma said.

Mary seemed to understand what that meant, as she went into a closet off the living room and pulled out two card tables, wiped them down, and went into the garage. "The chairs are in here. Help me bring them in."

As more people arrived, Kelly felt herself withdrawing. She smiled and answered direct questions, but didn't need to talk as much as everyone else did. As new children arrived, they looked at her suspiciously until their parents hugged and introduced her. Then they ran outside or down the stairs. They knew where the toys were.

"I'm carving the turkey," Da said. "Pick your places."

Kelly went to see if Ruth was awake. She was sitting on the bed, running her fingers through her hair.

"Show time," Kelly said. "I set you a place at the adults table next to Doug's daughter Bev. But I can move you to the kids table if you prefer."

Ruth laughed. Kelly was glad at least someone got her jokes.

The meal was a blur of noise and food and Ma getting up every few minutes for something, another serving spoon, more salt, butter, rolls, milk. Everything in abundance. Kelly sat between her single siblings, Greg a priest, and her youngest sister Annie, an adjunct instructor at a nearby community college. Greg and Annie argued over her about the role of women in the church.

"What do you think, Kelly," Annie said when they started discussing whether an all-male celibate priesthood created some of the problems the church currently faced.

Knowing better, but doing it anyway, she said, "I gave up on the church a long time ago."

The noise hushed, and everyone looked at her. Ruth smiled into her plate. Flustered, Ma raised her wine glass. "I'm glad everyone is here today. It's been a long time since all of my family has been together in the same room, and I am thankful."

Everyone raised their glasses, clinked with those nearest, and the din increased. Greg turned to talk with Doug.

"Sorry," Annie said. "I got caught up making my point and thought you'd be an ally."

"I do think women should be allowed in any profession, and I hope I'm an ally. But I'm pretty sure I can't talk theology with anyone. I don't want to."

"Then tell me about this big case you're working on. We were all pretty excited when we caught a glimpse of you in the crowd on the courthouse steps."

Da smiled at Kelly as she talked. He might even have been proud.

ANNIE AND DOUG'S family agreed to meet Kelly, Ruth, Ma, and Da in front of the old Marshall Field's, it was an abomination to call it Macy's, at eleven the next morning. Da parked in an underground lot, and the cold wind whipped when they reached the street. People crowded the windows along State Street, enjoying the elaborate decorations in each. Ruth stood back, seemingly unwilling to push herself to the front as the rest of them were doing.

"Can you see?" Kelly asked.

"Sort of," Ruth said.

"I can help get an opening for you."

"It's rude, Mom."

Kelly was taken aback. Everybody did it. It's how you got to the front. "I promise not to push or shove. Just slide between the elbows in whatever opening there is."

Ruth grimaced and shook her head.

"To the Christmas Market for bratwurst!" Annie said.

Red and white canopies filled Daly Plaza, the air heavy with the smell of cinnamon and sausages. The craft booths displayed ornaments, nuts, nutcrackers, beer steins, and nativity scenes. Kelly bought brats, strudel, and hot chocolate for herself and Ruth, balancing them as they walked.

"How about stockings and chocolates as souvenirs?" Kelly asked, and Ruth nodded. When they went to pay, Da pulled out his wallet.

"My treat," he said, putting an arm around each of them.

They ended the day watching their reflections in the Bean sculpture until it began to snow.

NINETEEN

KELLY OFFERED TO drive Therese to Vancouver for the annual First Nations Memorial March on Valentine's Day. This year, Diyanni was on the remembrance list. Kelly always meant to go, never got around to it, wasn't sure she'd be welcomed, was grateful to be invited. Ruth wanted to come too.

"Should I wear black, because it's kind of like a funeral?" Ruth asked from her bedroom.

"I don't think so. Red I think," Kelly said. "At least that's what I read in an article.

"Red because we're marching on Valentine's Day?" Ruth voice was filled with disbelief, but she put on a red shirt with her blue jeans. "That seems random."

Kelly smiled, glad she had a long, hooded red coat she could wear over her white blouse and navy wool pants. "No, not because it's Valentine's Day. The article said red is a symbol for the missing and murdered women and some indigenous people believe red is the only color the spirits can see. It talked about Red Dress Day, which started with an indigenous artist who put up red dresses around Canada to bring attention to all the missing. That's in May, though, which in my humble opinion seems like a better time for an outdoor march in Vancouver."

"Yeah, we're lucky snow isn't in the forecast today. Why is it today?"

Kelly shrugged. "I'm not sure. Apparently it's been held on Valentine's day since the 1990s."

"There must be a reason," Ruth said.

"Let's look it up later. Or ask Therese. Right now it's time to go." Kelly collected her keys and sunglasses from the kitchen counter and stuffed them in her purse.

Ruth gave Kelly a hug, something she seldom did. Kelly smiled and kissed Ruth's cheek.

"I have a maroon scarf if you want," Kelly said as Ruth put on her black pea coat.

Ruth nodded. "Good idea."

The morning was sunny, not too cold for February, and with little wind blowing from the Pacific. When they picked up Therese, Grandmother and Layla stood in the driveway waiting next to a basket filled with extra sweaters, parkas, signs, and a large folded sheet. Therese wore a red shawl over her parka and a long, loose black skirt with alternating red and white ribbons, while Grandmother and Layla were bundled in long wool coats over their red ribbon skirts. Black sweatpants tucked into boots peaked from under their skirts.

"Did Vern's mom make your necklace?" Kelly asked Therese when she noticed the beaded medicine bag she was wearing.

Therese touched the fringe on the pouch. "Yes. She gave it to me on the morning we brought Dee home. I've always had it in my drawer to keep it safe, but today I wanted to wear it."

Ruth and Layla loaded the trunk, and the five of them squeezed into Kelly's car.

Delays at the Canadian border made them later than they'd hoped. Therese seemed unperturbed, but first Ruth then Kelly became irritated, fidgety.

Several local streets in Vancouver were blocked off, and many of the parking lots were already full when they arrived. They rushed over broken sidewalks past boarded windows toward an old, restored, Carnegie Library, its mansard roof, tall columns, and gray brick exterior an architectural anomaly in an otherwise bleak neighborhood. They arrived at the family memorial ceremony just before it began. A Canadian First Nation elder with a long, thin braid at the door stepped in front of Kelly and Ruth.

Therese took Kelly's hand and said, "She's with us," and the man stepped back.

The room quieted when a young man near the front began hitting a drum and chanting softly. An older man with broad shoulders and a sun-wizened face stood at the podium until the song was finished and all was quiet.

"This is a sad day," the older man said. "We have come to honor our missing loved ones. We don't all speak the same language, but please speak your remembrance in whatever language seems best. We all understand in our hearts."

One by one, women and men remembered their daughters, mothers, aunts, cousins. Although Kelly didn't always understand the words, she felt their emotion as the families told about their children's lives, their spirits, how much they were missed. A young woman spoke with anger and grief about how long it took to find her sister, how she'd been ignored and forgotten by those who lived illegally on stolen ancestral lands and did not keep their promises of protection.

Therese was unable to speak, so Layla spoke for her. She spoke of her love for Diyanni and the reach and comfort of family during difficult times. "Dee was smart and beautiful and loyal. She made a couple of bad decisions, but she was young. I know she would have made it except for the violence of a man who did not know her. We will always miss her." Tears slipped down Layla's face, but her expression changed little. "We're thankful she was found even as we wish she'd been found alive. We grieve with all of you, especially those who still don't know what happened to your babies."

Kelly wiped the tears from her face with a tissue. She couldn't remember the last time she felt this hollow and sad. Ruth whispered she needed a tissue, and Kelly took one from the wad in her purse and handed it to her. She put her arms around Ruth's shoulders and felt her shaking.

The remembrances kept on. Fathers and mothers talking about their daughters. Men and women remembering their children. Some laughter, mostly sorrow. Expressions of grief, of helplessness, of anger. A heavy weight of despair overcame Kelly. So many. When no more relatives came to speak, an elderly man played a mournful song on a wooden flute.

As they left the building where the ceremony was held and stepped into the sunlight to join the march, Ruth said, "You see a lot of this kind of thing, don't you?"

Kelly nodded. "Mostly the domestic violence part, not usually the murders."

"Scares you, doesn't it?" Ruth asked.

"It does." Kelly felt they'd reached some sort of understanding.

Kelly found the Memorial March noticeably more somber than other protests she'd attended. No rock music, but plenty of chanting to the beat of rhythmic drums. A sad rather than angry sound. Nearly everyone wore something red, and many women wore cone-shaped woven hats over earmuffs or scarves. Instead of the angry slogans she'd seen at protest marches, the signs here were pictures of the missing or murdered. Layla handed Kelly and Ruth a picture of Diyanni attached to poster board with the words, "Never Forget." A few groups carried what looked like bedsheets with pictures of several women attached and others had quilts hand-embroidered with memorials. Kelly smelled burning and turned to see Grandmother with a smoldering stick of sage she waved in front of anyone who asked.

The crowd shifted and turned while they walked, often stopping to leave roses at places where women had been seen last, to pray, and to listen to short memories from the people who knew them. At one of these, Kelly saw Connor, alone and silent and with a stricken look on his face.

"Mrs. Hupt," Connor said, taking Therese's hands. "I'm so sorry."

"Thank you for all you've done," Therese said.

"Yes, thank you," Grandmother said as she walked around them with her sage, enveloping them in its smoke.

"I'm sad and angry," Connor waived a pamphlet that listed the names of the missing and murdered women. "Almost nine hundred. Probably more since this was printed. How can we stop it?"

No one had an answer.

Connor walked next to Kelly for the rest of the march, joined hands with them at the healing circle in Oppenheimer Park. He said goodbye when the crowd headed toward the community meal.

"I'd like to keep the task force going," Connor said. "Will you still be a part of it?"

"Sure, but just include me in the meetings when there's a specific legal question or issue."

"Good idea." Connor hesitated. "Will you meet me for lunch once in a while?"

"Let's keep in touch," Kelly said. "Friends?"

Connor looked relieved and squeezed her gloved hand. "Friends."

"He's nice looking," Ruth said to Kelly when Connor disappeared into the crowd. "You interested?"

"We're friends," Kelly said. "That's all."

When they arrived at the feast, the tables with the best food were mobbed, but they each were able to grab a few apples and unidentified jerky.

"I'd like to stop along the bay on the way home," Therese said to Kelly. "Can we?"

"Sure, but if you want it to still be light, we'd better get going."

Kelly took them through a drive-through near the Canadian border and made it to Galmenberg Bay near the mouth of the Hotsaem just before the sun set. An orange haze lined horizon as Therese led them toward the water's edge. When they reached the shore, Grandmother took out her sage. Therese pulled a small picture of Diyanni from her purse.

"Dee loved this beach, so I thought remembering her here too was important," Therese said.

Therese lit the remains of the sage and let it burn on a shell on the sand next to the picture. No one said anything. They watched the dusk settle into night and the tide rise.

When it was almost too dark to see, Therese put a pinch of sage ash and Diyanni's picture into the medicine bag she was wearing, then scattered the remaining ash into the sea.

CLOUDS SCUTTLED PAST the moon as Traveler scrambled through the brush along the river's bank. Nights were long and cold again, full of windless sound and icy water rushing over rocks and fallen trees. Only the night animals kept him company. He ran until he saw light outlining a small hill long before the morning birds started calling.

Traveler crept along the edge of a large expanse of blacktop, dodging the pools of light that marked the border between human and forest. He remembered the pain that dark night long ago, didn't want to provoke the now silent machines lined in a row, their round eyes dark, into chasing him again. He didn't look back until he hid behind tall bushes at the top of the hill far from the great building and its flashing lights of many colors. Three humans scuffled in the darkest corner of the asphalt, far from the moving vehicles and the building's staccato noise. One human opened the door of a van, another shoved the third into a dark space. Even at this distance Traveler heard whimpering and smelled blood. One man pulled the door shut while the other started the motor. The van's round eyes shone toward Traveler, then followed the line of cars near the building onto the dark road on the other side.

Traveler ran as fast as he could toward home. His girls would be looking for him, would need his protection.

ACKNOWLEDGMENTS

I wrote this book as a part of a community of writers with the Writing by Writers *Draft* program, and am grateful for the guidance from my mentors, Joshua Mohr, Pam Houston, and Samantha Dunn, and the critiques of my cohort members, Julia Poole, Nancy Parshall, Meri Johnston, Annie Lareau, Catherine Cooper, Susan Baller-Shepard, Diz Warner, Mitzi Scott, July Westhale, Natalie Ponte, Andrea Leeb, Alyssa Swanson Hamilton, Beth McLaughlin, and Michelle Geoga. Although I missed the face to face discussions after the pandemic forced our conversations onto video conferences and email, your attentiveness and friendship helped me through the gloom of the lockdown and after. Thank you, too, to Karen Nelson whose encouragement and skill made this wonderful experience work.

Thanks to everyone at Bedazzled Ink Publishing for helping me get my novel into the world, and especially to Elizabeth Gibson for her enthusiasm for *Flotsam* and her helpful responses to all my questions and to my editor C. A. Casey for her attention to detail and for helping make *Flotsam* a better book.

I acknowledge that the subject matter of this novel is a sensitive topic that deals with a matter of great importance, the many missing and murdered women of the Indigenous and First Nation communities. I know that as an older white woman who has had little exposure to Indigenous people I may have inadvertently offended someone. I am grateful for the guidance of my sensitivity reader, Stacey Parshall Jensen, who alerted me to issues I was unable to see, and did so with firmness and kindness. I admit that I did not take all her suggestions, and any insensitivity in my novel is completely my fault. I apologize for any offense I may have given.

Thank you to my friends and family who read drafts and talked me through ideas and who encouraged me when I felt like giving up, especially my daughters Jen and Stacy, my sisters-in-law Joyce and Ann, my brother Dave, my nephew Mike, Jennifer Pingeon, Margaret Wilson, Fredda Bisman, Donna Bronski, Marilyn Pollard, Carol Benyi, and Jean Updike. And thank you to Kelly Dwyer and my classmates in her Iowa Summer Writing Festival Class, especially Christine Javid with whom I had many discussions about being sensitive when writing about other cultures. Thanks also to David Heska Wanbli Weiden and the workshop members at the Tucson Festival of Books Master Class whose helpful comments prodded me to finally finish the novel.

I am grateful for everyone's insights, suggestions, and encouragement.

Patricia Boomsma is a retired Arizona lawyer now writing full time. She earned a master's degree in English from Purdue University, a law degree from Indiana University in Indianapolis, and an MFA in Creative Writing from Queens University in Charlotte. Her publications include short stories in *Scarlet Leaf Review, Persimmon Tree*, and *Vignette Review. Indolent Press* published her poem "Arc of the Apocalypse" both online and in the anthology "Poems From the Aftermath." Her first novel, *The Way of Glory* (Edeleboom Books 2018), won the Bill Fisher Award for Best First Book-Fiction from the Independent Book Publishers Association and a First Place/Best in Category Chaucer Award from Chanticleer Book Reviews. Her second novel, *Lost*, is scheduled for publication by Bedazzled Ink in 2024.

Visit Patricia's website: https://patboomsma.com

Printed in the USA
CPSIA information can be obtained
at www.ICGtesting.com
LVHW040759060923
757193LV00005B/31

9 781960 373120